NUN
MASSACRE

A NOVELIZATION

PUPPET COMBO ®
&
REGINA WATTS

Concept & Original Video Game: Vague Scenario LLC
Text: Regina Watts
Typesetting: M. F. Sullivan
Cover: Mateo Jakičević

Puppet Combo® Online: https://puppetcombo.com
Regina Watts Online: https://hrhdegenetrix.com

PROLOGUE

SISTER EUPHEMIA WAS as afraid of Mother Apollonia as the children were. Maybe more.

A floorboard creaked and the young nun froze. Her stomach tightened with dread. She held her breath and listened to the halls of the school, begging for more information.

Euphemia didn't want to gossip about the Mother Superior. The truth was, she wouldn't have told a soul how she felt...but she didn't have to. It was all over her face when Mother Apollonia's heavy footsteps marched past her office or stormed down the stairs. Things got to be so bad that Euphemia found herself creeping around the school as though she were a student. Always listening for the slightest footfall that might alert her to Apollonia's arrival.

If the Lord saw fit to watch out for her in such a time, Euphemia could sneak into an empty classroom or dart down a hall—anywhere out of the path of the Mother Superior. It wasn't that Euphemia was in any way lazy: she did a great deal of work around the school. Far more than some of her fellow Sisters.

Yet nothing she did could please the elder nun, who, seeing Euphemia pausing to watch the birds through a window, would snap her fingers as though the younger nun were a dog. While, blushing, Euphemia jumped to attention, Apollonia might say something like, "Idle hands, Sister! I noticed you haven't dusted the bookshelves in the western wing for some time."

That wasn't so bad...but it could get bad.

For some reason, with the children, it was always bad.

Euphemia truly despised watching Apollonia interact with their students. The old witch ignored the children completely until she was in a foul mood. Then, much as with the nuns, the person on whom her cold eye landed became subject to her heinous whims.

And this didn't even include the classes she taught: Euphemia heard rumors that Apollonia's unlucky pupils were particularly maltreated.

But Euphemia didn't like to dwell on these things. Who did? Bad things happened to everyone in life, after all...the best thing was to simply soldier on. To provide the gentle influence the children needed to balance out Apollonia's harsh tutelage.

The Good Lord had put Euphemia there for just such a purpose, no doubt. There was no sense in doing something as outrageous as reporting the foul behavior.

2

After all...if she worked hard, kept improving her relationship with God, and didn't rock the Church's boat, Euphemia might be Mother Superior after Apollonia died. Then the convent and the school it ran would be capable of some reform! Wouldn't that be nice. What a bastion of Godly education it would be!

Until then, it would resemble its present custodian: grim and bleak, its somewhat dim halls rendered all the more frighteningly dark beginning with the earliest hours of each night.

Someday, school. Someday!

It, like the children and like Euphemia, would just have to get through the final years of Apollonia's life. Until then, Euphemia would remain skittish: frozen in hallways, looking for an escape route, her breath held to catch the sound of Apollonia's footsteps.

Another floorboard creaked.

Euphemia released the breath she'd been holding. That step was much too light to belong to the Mother Superior!

Crossing herself, Euphemia resumed her usual evening path through the school and continued extinguishing lights as she went. She paused by a bathroom and, leaning in, snapped off the switch for the night.

When she leaned back out, who should be standing at the hallway's end but little Janie McDonnell.

"Goodness, Janie!" Euphemia laughed, her hand upon her suddenly racing heart. "You scared me."

"Oh," said the girl, her tone listless with exhaustion after another long day in the halls of St. Cecilia's. "Sorry. I thought you were Mother Apollonia."

With a light laugh, Sister Euphemia shook her

head. "There's a frightful thought!"

Janie smiled weakly at the kinder nun's conspiratorial camaraderie. It was an unnerving smile. The girl's lips moved, but her blue eyes—vast orbs once full of light—did not.

Those eyes were not the only things that had changed during Janie's time in the school. Her very face had lost the glow of childhood. At nine, the adolescent had already achieved the grim aura of adults.

Suddenly overcome with a spate of nervousness, Euphemia reminded herself that she was the only adult in the hall at the moment.

"Now, Janie," she said with a glance around, "you know you ought to be in bed right now."

"Yes," said Janie in that same soft tone, her hollow voice drifting off like the wind.

"Did you need something?"

Janie didn't answer.

It was odd. She had become very quiet these days, but even by Janie's standards, she was acting withdrawn. Sister Euphemia shared a glance with the jolly clown doll clutched in the girl's arm.

Was Janie sleepwalking? Her eyes were open, but Euphemia had heard that some people could sleepwalk—even sleeptalk—very convincingly. Perhaps the staff needed to keep an eye on her at night. Euphemia put a kindly hand on Janie's shoulder and tried to urge her away.

Janie stayed so still she might as well have been a statue.

"Come along, Janie...Janie!" Laughing despite herself, (a nervous laugh, a high bird's laugh somehow pleading in its twittering), Euphemia said unsteadily,

"Aren't you just a little Saint Lucy! Rooted right to the spot..."

At last, a true smile twisted across the girl's features. A dimple appeared in her cheek as she turned to look eagerly into Euphemia's face. Here was a hint of the Janie who first came through those boarding school doors a mere handful of months before: bright and high-spirited and more than a little giddy. All the qualities that tended to get children sent to schools like this one.

"I love Saint Lucy," enthused the girl. "She's my favorite. They wanted to do bad things to her, huh, Sister Euphemia?"

"They did," said Euphemia sadly, finally getting Janie into motion. Hand lightly on Janie's shoulder, the nun guided her toward the stairs and the floor where the students slept. "Yes, indeed. They wanted to take her to a place where her life would no longer be her own, and where her body would be subject to terrible things. But she wanted to devote her body and soul to Christ."

"So instead"—Janie's beaming grin never faltered, and Euphemia found it extremely unnerving—"she pulled out her own eyes! Right, Sister Euphemia? And then she put them on a plate, like how you showed us in that painting."

For some reason, such a sentence sent a strange bolt of guilt running through the nun. But, why...what could be inappropriate about teaching the children the lives of the Catholic martyrs?

It was part of their curriculum. The nuns did their best to explain everything in an age-appropriate fashion, of course, but when all was said and done the children were going to hear the stories at some point. It had might as well be introduced early in their education. Then they might spend a lifetime closely acquainted with the miraculous gifts God bestowed upon believers willing to sacrifice their bodies in the name of the faith.

"That's true," agreed Euphemia as they made it to the landing of the stairs. "Some sources say she gouged out her own eyes, and some say somebody else did it to punish her. But, you know—when they went to bury her, they discovered the Lord had restored her eyes!"

Janie laughed wildly at that. Euphemia's diaphragm tightened with panic. Apollonia would hear the girl for sure.

Euphemia paused there on the landing to listen as closely as she could. At the same time, she asked the girl, "Just what's so funny?"

"Because! What good are her eyes when she's *dead?*"

The hallway in the floor above them creaked. One step: then another. Heavy, determined; drawn by the sound of a child's laughter.

All the blood drained from Euphemia's face.

Oblivious, Janie went on with a shake of her head, "If God wanted anybody to listen to Him, He should have kept Lucy from going through all that in the first place! Or, if it had to be that way, He should have made the eyeballs of the people torturing her fall out! Or explode."

The girl added this last thought with a morbid laugh.

Euphemia was too busy panicking to pay her any attention now. Mother Apollonia was coming right this way, and here they were on the stairs!

Oh, how could she turn them around without Janie noticing some ill feelings within the convent of the school? It wasn't appropriate for the students to know how Euphemia and the others feared Apollonia...yet fight or flight had a powerful hold on the human mind.

Euphemia was just in the process of turning Janie around without worrying about an explanation when, to her horror, Mother Apollonia's harsh tone cut through the peals of Janie's laughter.

"Janie? Is that you?"

Euphemia's eyes squeezed shut.

Exhaling, the young nun forced herself to call, "And me, Mother Apollonia!"

The pace of the footsteps increased. By some miracle, Sister Euphemia managed to produce a smile. Apollonia appeared at the top of the staircase.

"Well! There's *one* of our teachers...I have no idea where the other Sisters are lurking about tonight. Just what are you doing here with Janie, Euphemia? Did you find her wandering around again?"

"If God really cared about me," Janie said to Apollonia, her laughter snapping off like a light and her demeanor growing ice cold, "He would make your eyes explode."

Euphemia's stomach flipped. The mouths of babes, as it was said!

Mother Apollonia's eyes didn't explode, but they did bug from her head. Her thin lips falling open in a great 'O' of shock, Apollonia seemingly struggled to process this suggestion.

Euphemia, catching Janie by the shoulders, looked at the girl and tried to figure out if she understood what she'd just done. "Now, Janie! That's not a very nice thing to—"

"You come with me right this instant! Euphemia, get away from her."

"Oh, but Mother Apollonia, I think she's just tir—"

Apollonia's backhanded slap was as quick as the bite of a cobra. A flame exploded across Euphemia's face and was quickly followed by a wave of overwhelming numbness. Eyes filling with tears against the pain and humiliation, Euphemia stumbled back from the child.

One hand unconsciously pressed to her stinging cheek.

"If she's tired, she'd ought to have stayed in bed... come with me, you little brat."

With a claw-like grip, Apollonia snatched Janie by the wrist and dragged her down the stairs.

Euphemia knew what was next. Soon the two would be behind the door of Apollonia's office...then, through the frosted glass, all manner of terrible cries would pierce Euphemia's heart.

Ah! Why did she respond when Apollonia called out?

"Don't worry, Sister Euphemia," said Janie over her shoulder before being pulled out of sight. With her free hand, she waved her clown toy. "Even if God won't protect me, Bongo will."

Then Janie was gone, and so was Apollonia.

Euphemia could breathe again, but not without shame to think of what Janie now endured. Inspecting her fingers to make sure no skin had broken, Euphemia considered returning to the bathroom to investigate her face...but, if no blood was to be seen, there was really nothing to be done. She'd put some ice on it once she made sure the dormitory lights were out.

What had Apollonia been doing upstairs? Whatever it was, the answer wasn't turning off lights. Euphemia shook her head in annoyance. What did the woman do around there? Other than frighten children, of course. Well! Someday, when Euphemia was Mother Superior...

Sister Euphemia barely had time to spiral into her usual grandiose thoughts of self-justification for her complicity in child abuse. She stepped past the dormitory where Janie generally slept. Seeing as the light was off, Euphemia would have ignored it if she hadn't stepped in something wet.

The nun stepped back, glancing down at the wet hem of her habit. Water? What could be leaking from that room? Did a pipe burst somewhere? Or—maybe it was the doing of that new air conditioning system.

Euphemia knelt and pressed her hand to the wet substance.

She inspected her fingertips to find them painted crimson.

Her mind almost wouldn't comprehend what it saw.

Blood? Blood! Oozing out from beneath the dormitory door.

Surely, it couldn't be. Yet—yet, as her mind scrambled through possible alternate explanations, it found nothing. No way to explain the growing pool of vital fluid steadily flooding out of the room where a quarter of the students slept.

Breath held, desperate to see the source of this substance, Sister Euphemia kept to one side of the pool. She pushed open the door.

Twenty dead students bled in their beds or upon the floor.

The sight drew a scream from Sister Euphemia that was so loud, so high and fearful, that it seemed to come from somewhere else. She had never heard herself scream that way: never felt as though she were dreaming because she was simply so panicked that there was no room in her brain for anything but unconscious survival mechanisms.

Dead! Truly dead. Each and every one of them lay still, drenched in blood, their throats slit or their nightgowns seeping through from multiple stab wounds. All these lives were no more: everything about the future that had been so certain just was now taken away forever. Plans were reduced to failed dreams. Parents, to mourners.

Euphemia, to a madwoman—or very nearly. Though tears streamed down her face and baleful sobs wracked her frame, she retained sense enough to step back from the blood and look around.

A phone! She needed a phone. Mother Apollonia had access to the only telephone in the building. Forgetting her fear of the old woman right away, Janie rushed down the stairs. Her heart pounded in her ears and, drawing her hem a few inches higher to avoid tripping, the nun prayed that whatever had happened to that dormitory had not happened to the rest. There would be time to check when the police were on their way.

Mother Apollonia's office stood oddly quiet, a square of light pouring out into the darkened hallway through the frosted glass window. Euphemia tried the knob and, finding it locked, jiggled it rapidly while pounding her fist upon the wooden frame of the door.

"Mother Apollonia! Please, I must talk to you this instant—let me use the phone, oh, please, it's an emergency—"

Apollonia's habit appeared in silhouette, visible on

the other side of the office through the frosted glass window. Heart leaping, Euphemia managed, "The children," before the lock opened for her.

Beneath the constant tries of her hand, the door swung wide.

Euphemia was as unready for that as she was for the corpse on the floor before Apollonia's desk.

The body was almost unrecognizable, its screaming mouth and empty red eye sockets like a set of variations on the same fleshy orifice. Crimson rivers of thick blood had swirled with the gore of ocular matter, a viscous pink face paint over the cadaver's cheeks.

Its eternal scream seemed to predict the one Euphemia produced while her hands flew over her mouth.

Desperate to look anywhere but the body, her eyes lifted to the phone. Like an automaton programmed for one goal, Euphemia stepped toward the desk where it sat.

She snatched the receiver off the base, which fell to reveal its line had been physically cut.

A floorboard creaked behind Euphemia.

The metal of a knife plunged into the back of her shoulder, the cold blade curiously hot as it impaled her flesh and plowed her deltoid in two. At once unable to move her left arm, the pain so overwhelming she could no longer think straight, Euphemia collapsed forward and away from her assailant.

Somehow, its removal was even more painful than its insertion—but the same could not be said of the second stab, or the third. Hot blood lapped across the floor as the knife punctured her lungs, pierced between her ribs, severed her vertebrae to send an unbearable scream of lightning agony racing down her calves and into her skull. That one was so bad she vomited a little, her sobs turning into gags and thereafter into an inescapable retch as she began to choke.

"You didn't have to look," said the nun's attacker, pulling Euphemia's veil from her soft blonde locks and gripping her by the hair that had once been a source of pride—that had once attracted praise from other women and longing looks from boys.

What had happened to those days? Where had all the time gone?

Why had Euphemia spent so much of it here, belittled and abused by Apollonia?

The flesh of her throat pulled apart at the blade's behest. Blood splattered down Euphemia's black habit and over the front of the desk. When her killer dropped her she managed to stay upright, her cheek pressing to the cool surface of the wood.

A tear rolled down Euphemia's cheek, mingling with the blood and the vomit.

The killer shut the door.

1978

1.

DAWN FOOLED AROUND with the knob of Barbara's radio until Andrea leaned forward and slapped her hand.

"Would you cut it out and pick something already? We'll *be* there by the time you've settled on a station!"

"I can't help it! If I hear "Night Fever" one more time I'm going to throw myself over these cliffs."

While Barb laughed, Mary scowled sullenly from beside Andrea in the back of the car. "Some of us *like* the Bee Gees, Dawn."

"Some of us just like fun," Andrea agreed, pushing her honey-colored ponytail back over her shoulder.

"You need to stop trying to be too cool all the time, Dawn."

Scoffing, Dawn adjusted the wire frames of her glasses. "I can't help that I like interesting music. This stuff they're always playing on the radio just isn't interesting. It's all dance music! I don't like to dance."

Mary repressed a smirk. She turned toward the darkness of the storm, her face against the glass and her eyes glued to the black clouds responsible for the relentless rain.

"Maybe if you had somebody to dance with, you'd like it more—but most of us put ourselves out there on the floor and have fun whether we're single or not. It's just about the beat, you know?"

There was no point in defending her opinion that this was the real problem with disco…it wouldn't do anything but aggravate the people around her. Dawn couldn't help it, though. She was obsessed with music and was widely known as, well, sort of a total nerd. Too busy for boys or other forms of extracurricular amusement, she had thrown herself into her art and was spending one last summer at home before going off to Juilliard on a well-earned scholarship.

Given how outrageously busy she kept herself by working on new compositions, studying existing ones and laboring part-time at a local instrument repair shop, it was a miracle Barbie had ever noticed her.

But that was just how Barbara was. One of those insanely perfect people: the nice sort of young woman who became president of the Drama Club, took all the advanced drawing classes, had at least twice been in the student council, kept a boyfriend, and still managed to go to parties and remember everybody's name.

Dawn always had it in her head that somebody so Type A was bound to be a bully. Upon getting to know Barb during Drama Club, however, Dawn had to admit there was something genuinely magnetic about her personality...and genuine was the word. Barbara was one of the nicest people Dawn had ever known—she never had a mean word to say about anyone, and once she became somebody's friend, that was that.

With graduation having passed, Dawn had expected Barbara to stop talking to her altogether; and it was true that both girls saw less of each other. But when Barbara and her boyfriend, Kevin, decided to throw a party to mark the start of summer, Dawn was one of the first people she called.

So, even though Mary and Andrea were a little more stuck-up, (a cheerleader and a volleyball player, respectively), Dawn found herself looking forward to the night for more than a week. There had been promises of good-looking guys, most of them single, as well as beer and various other recreational activities.

However...this storm, which seemed to increase in violence as Barb's car crawled up the treacherous mountain path to the fast beat of her windshield wipers, did not bode well for Dawn's love-life.

"Do you really think people are going to risk coming all the way up here in a storm like this?"

At Dawn's question, Mary shook her curly red mane and enthused, "I was just thinking the same *thing!* How's anybody supposed to *see* in rain like this? Look: you can barely see the boys' taillights."

It was true. With the beating rain and blackened sky, the red lights that Barbara followed were far from their brightest. Taking it slow, her hands at ten and two, Barbie was nonetheless constantly making adjustments to compensate for a slight drift this way or that. Dawn tried not to be too nervous...but Andrea, laughing as she leaned forward, didn't make it easy.

"Come on! Do you think people are willing to miss a party at a spooky place like St. Cecilia's Preparatory School? This was such a cool idea, Barbie."

Dawn couldn't help but think Barbara bore more resemblance to Farrah Fawcett than any doll, yet the nickname still fit her somehow. While Barb smiled at it, she said, "Well, I hope it'll turn out well—but I'm worried that Mary's right. Who's going to want to come out here in rain like this?"

Heart sinking, Dawn said, "You mean—"

"Looks like it's just gonna be us."

Barb's admission made Dawn collapse back in her seat with a disappointed sigh. Another missed opportunity! At this rate she was going to end up in Juilliard without even having held a boy's hand.

"Don't be sad, Dawn!" Barb reached over and patted her hand, drawing her out of her sulk. "We'll still have fun."

"You guys will! With your boyfriends. Meanwhile I'll just be hanging out...the seventh wheel...ugh!" Resisting her urge to fiddle with the radio, Dawn stuck her hands under her thighs and asked, "What's so special about this place, anyway?"

Andrea gasped with delight. Leaning forward again, the jock asked, "Oh, St. Cecilia's Preparatory School? You mean that you don't *know?*"

Dawn rolled her eyes. As she twisted in her seat, a few strands of straight brown hair fell across her cheek. Dawn blew them out of her way and asked, "Let me guess—it's haunted?"

"People don't know! They say nobody's survived a

night there."

"Okay," said Dawn with a laugh and a sidelong look at Barb. "So the natural thing is to have a party?"

Waving her hand, Barbara said, "Oh, come on, it's just a silly urban legend...I was really hoping that we'd be able to set up outside and see the stars. Seemed like a nice place to have a good time without bothering anybody else, at least."

Always one to take the bait on something like this, Dawn found herself asking Andrea, "And what happens to people who stay the night, exactly?"

"Well..." With a cheesy wiggle of her eyebrows, Andrea explained, "St. Cecilia's was renowned for its ability to take even the most hardened juvenile delinquent and turn her into a good, God-fearing young lady...but then, one night, there was an incident."

Barbara turned the radio off as Dawn asked, "What kind of incident?"

"A massacre," answered Andrea. "All the students, teachers—everyone was killed. Stabbed to death and left to die floating in their own blood."

Dawn balked at this. "You must be kidding."

"I'm totally not—in fact, they never figured out who did it. Some people think a maniac broke in and killed everyone that night, but it's hard to say. On top of all that, one of the kids went missing, and so did one of the nuns...the Mother Superior, I think."

"Say," said Mary, who had been listening to all this quietly and now looked a bit pale, "you don't think it's, like, those gnarly *Satanists* or anything like that, do you?"

"That's what some people say," Andrea continued, her eyes bright with lurid delight to relate a tale of such horror. "They think the girl and the nun were taken to be part of some kind of crazy occult ritual— sacrificed, you know. The rumor is that the nun is still seen wandering the halls, looking for her dead body...or the person who killed her. She's the one responsible for all the deaths of people trying to stay overnight, I'll bet."

"Far out," said Mary earnestly.

Dawn rolled her eyes.

"That's the stupidest thing I've ever heard," the music student told them. "Who could ever think there's truth to a thing like that? I don't even know if I believe a massacre happened there."

Slapping a hand upon the back of Dawn's seat, Andrea insisted, "It's true! You can look up the articles next time you're at the library. Something like sixty people, students and staff members, lost their lives that night."

Dawn was only about to ask for a few more details when Barb's car came to a sudden stop.

While the compact rumbled in place, Barbara put it into park. To Dawn's surprise, she grabbed her umbrella and got out of the car.

Straightening out in her seat, Dawn peered through the rain-covered windshield. The boys' car had come to a stop, it seemed, for reasons that were obscured by the weather. Barb's boyfriend, Kevin, stood outside of the covered Jeep with his hands on his hips. When Barbara came up behind him, they carried on a brief conversation during which Mary and Andrea leaned forward to see.

Mary looked over at Dawn. "What's the problem?"

Just as Dawn was shaking her head, Barb's conversation with Kevin ended. Still beneath the shelter of her umbrella, she returned to the driver's side of the car and let herself in. Water splashed across all of them as she had to leave the door open a few seconds to shake off the umbrella, a fruitless effort amid the driving rain over which she raised her voice.

"Kevin says the road's out," explained Barbie. While the women in the back seat moaned with annoyance and settled into their respective places with a shared look of disappointment, Barbara slid into the car and shut the door behind her. At a more reasonable volume, she continued, "He says his Jeep can make it over the mud that's left, but it'll be cramped."

"What about the turntable?" Mary looked over her shoulder, toward the trunk. "We can't bring it out in the rain."

"Then we'll have to make do with what music we can find when we're there...maybe there'll be something."

With that winning smile bright even in the given circumstances, Barbara turned to gauge Dawn's opinion.

"Well, Dawn? Should we roll with the punches?"

Did she really have a choice? Something gnawing at Dawn's insides said that turning back then and there might have kept the night from being—what? Cursed?

She was being ridiculous. How could she let a scary story get to her? It was kid stuff. Shaking her head, Dawn opened her mouth to agree that they could all squeeze into the Jeep with a bit of work.

Lightning pierced the sky; seconds later, thunder.

2.

THE CHUNK OF road that had slid away from the hillside did not bode well for the journey. Dawn pondered her decision as the seven high school graduates bounced around together in Kevin's Jeep. With Kevin driving, Barb had been offered the only free space available; and slim Dawn, being unattached, was forced by circumstance to perch upon her friend's knees.

Well...there were worse fates in the world, Dawn supposed. Her glance darted away from Barb's smile as their eyes met. At least Barb didn't cover herself in cologne like the boys did. Scott, up in the passenger seat beside Kevin, had Mary in his lap. Whatever he wore managed to make Dawn sneeze at least once, since she and Barbie were in the seat behind.

Andrea, meanwhile, snuggled up with Chris, an effect that was somewhat funny given that the athletic young woman was a hair taller than her quiet, slightly nerdy boyfriend. She managed to knock her head a fair few times on the cover of the Jeep, and each time everybody laughed.

Everybody except Dawn, who could only manage a nervous smile.

"What's the matter, Dawn?"

Barbara's question, though gently phrased and meant, was addressed to Dawn in front of the whole car. She had no choice but to say, "Oh, nothing! Just got a little damp, that's all."

"Well, we'll be there soon." Fiddling with the headlights and trying a few other settings before giving up and ending where he started, Kevin squinted through the torrential downpour. "I don't think I've seen rain like this since I was a kid!"

"It really is coming down tonight." With a sigh, Barbara glanced out at the sky as if searching for a moon. Instead, she received another whiplash of lightning. "It's too bad that we'll be the only ones, but it might still be fun...we'll have to stay the night for sure!"

Dawn couldn't help but laugh. "You seem almost excited!"

"Aren't you?" Grinning, shrugging, Barbara said, "It's an adventure!"

That was one way of putting it, anyway.

The Jeep, having navigated past the narrowed section of road without causing any more of a landslide, managed to climb the rest of the way to St. Cecilia's Preparatory School without further incident. In fact, by the time they were up there, the rain had eased somewhat. A sense of optimism established itself. Maybe a few friends would make it after all?

Dawn wasn't sure she wanted them to, in truth. As the Jeep slowly rounded the last bend, the school building came into view. A chill rushed down Dawn's spine.

"There it is," said Barb, her tone bright as though she'd seen a celebrity. "Oh, what a beautiful building!"

For a certain definition of beautiful. Maybe it had been, once. But, being neglected as it had been for something like thirty years, St. Cecilia's Preparatory School was falling apart. The weed-riddled grounds were covered in bricks and debris, and not just from the school.

Trash was scattered around, and the sight of it actually put Dawn at ease. So others had been here... plenty of others, from the looks of it. Maybe homeless people used this place to sleep sometimes. Hikers, maybe, coming up the mountain and passing through the area. The teenagers would have to be careful, of course, but surely there was nothing to worry about.

Not that she was worried, of course.

Dawn pushed away her feeling as Kevin parked the Jeep. The teenagers all remained where they were, leaning forward, staring up at the looming black building that glowered coldly down at them. The tall windows arranged along the façade were bleak and dark, revealing no hint of the rooms inside.

Only the assurance that, whatever they expected to find there, they would be wrong.

They would be better off not going on.

They would be better off turning around and—

"I got the beer," said Kevin, cramming his keys into his pocket and climbing out of the Jeep.

One pair at a time, the remaining teenagers followed suit. First, Scott and Mary; then, Chris and Andrea.

Dawn moved to get out. Barb caught her hand.

"Do you want me to have Kevin drive you home?"

Almost laughing, Dawn said, "It took us over an hour to get here! Think how long it'll be before he gets back."

"That doesn't matter. I want you to have a good time. If you don't feel safe, it's important that we get you home."

There was a definite temptation there. That same intuition that had been buzzing in her mind all night now nudged Dawn as though to indicate now would be her last chance to turn around and exit the situation.

All the same, Barb's kindness moved her. How could she disappoint her friend during their final summer before college? She smiled and shook her head.

"I'm really fine, Barb. I guess I'm just confused—what's so cool about this place?"

"I've always wanted to see it! I love creepy stories like the ones they tell about this place. And with everyone going away to college, you and me and so many other people going out of state, well..."

For once, Barbara's cheerful expression faded into a complex and distant look of meditation. She shook her head. "Anyway...I had a great aunt or something who worked here while all that stuff happened. Sister Euphemia—she was a nun. I guess I just want to see if I can meet a ghost."

Dawn, laughing, said, "I didn't know you were into stuff like this."

Somebody called from the door of the building.

"You guys coming?"

Kevin's voice was only barely audible over the renewing storm.

"Looks like it's starting up again," observed Barb, sighing heftily and opening the door for Dawn. "I sure do know how to pick a date!"

A date, and a location.

The school was pitch black as they entered. With the front doors boarded up, the teens had lugged their beer around the side of the building and found another entrance. This smaller door yielded at once and opened into a hallway that, though flooded with some of the thickest darkness imaginable, was still infinitely dryer than even the covered Jeep had been.

Everyone sighed in relief. While Chris dug out a Zippo to shed a little light on the subject, the ladies shook out their hair.

Scott and Kevin peered around in the darkness. "Man," remarked Scott, water sluicing from the gelled hair that no longer looked quite so styled, "guess this place doesn't have any power, huh?"

"Why would it, numbnuts? It's been abandoned for years." Shaking his head, Kevin looked for a light of his own. He came up with a pocket flashlight attached to his keys. With their combined lights they discerned the wainscoting, the corner of the hallway—and, beyond that, a set of stairs. Looking down the long, dark hall, he grumbled, "They might have a generator somewhere, though, since they're so far from town."

"What was that about 'numbnuts,'" muttered Scott, bumping shoulders with Kevin on his way down the hall. "You guys didn't bring lanterns or anything?"

Barbara sighed. "We did, but there just wasn't room in Kevin's Jeep for it...not with all of us and the beer."

"Priorities," said Kevin agreeably.

While everybody else laughed, they paused at the staircase. His flashlight's weak beam shone on the first flight and the landing where it ended, a spiral of dust caught in the illumination between ominous slices of darkness. A door's handle invited them deeper into the building.

Kevin led the way to it, continuing aloud, "There's got to be a gymnasium or something around here..."

A dining hall, actually. It was, after all, a boarding school dedicated to the refinement and re-education of young ladies, and therefore bore some similarities to a college...or a prison.

They found it fairly quickly, trying the metal door off of the landing to find yet another dark hallway. Each side was lined with offices, and at the far end loomed a juncture with several options: left, right, or another imposing set of stairs with landings cloaked in shadow. They decided to head to the right and, at the end of this second hall, managed to find the broad dining hall doors already open.

"Say," cried Barb, hurrying forward as Kevin's flashlight illuminated the largest space they'd yet to find, "this place is great! Just what we needed."

"A little trashed," Dawn couldn't help but note.

In the absence of students to feed, the neglected place had become a storage unit. Boxes were stacked everywhere; more dust motes pranced through the beam of the flashlight; a rat's wormlike tail vanished through a hole in the floorboards. Another entrance to the room seemed to indicate a path all the way around the school, but who knew if that door even worked?

The third exit led to a kitchen, its great swinging

double doors shut and a window in them missing its glass.

"Oh, come on. With a little re-organizing, this place is a perfect dance floor. It's fun," insisted Barb.

Dawn wandered over to peer into the dark kitchen. The industrial-sized scale, barely reflecting the occasional pass of the faint flashlight beam, seemed fit to weigh a person. It made Dawn shudder as her friend went on, "Rustic!"

"You know," said Andrea, "I'm with Barb. This place is perfect for us! Some music and some lights, and we've got ourselves a party...if anyone shows up, anyway."

"I wonder if there's any kind of radio or anything around here?" Mary pondered the question aloud, searching uselessly through the darkness but clearly unwilling to actually touch anything lest she disturb a spider or another rat.

"I can go look," Scott began, but his girlfriend grabbed his arm with a noise of protest.

"No, Scott! Don't leave me here...it's too creepy. Let somebody else go!"

Andrea rolled her eyes. "Totally lame. Chris, how about you go?"

But Chris, with a few quick glances toward the darkness that represented the rough position of the doorway, shook his head. "Me? No way—it's the 20th century. Why should I have to go wandering out into that darkness just because I'm a guy?"

"Oh my God." Andrea almost laughed but instead left it at, "You're kidding, right?"

While Andrea and Chris fell into soft bickering, Dawn cleared her throat.

"Uh," she said, "I can go—it's no big deal. This place

is falling apart, but it doesn't seem like I'm going to fall through the floorboards or anything."

Barbara, visibly thrilled that there might be a way for her party to come together, rushed over and took Dawn's hands. "Really? You wouldn't mind? Oh, I sure appreciate it. Chris? Could you let her borrow your Zippo?"

While Dawn accepted it, Barb suggested, "Maybe try those offices along the hall there—they might have something. This place was sealed up and condemned once the investigation was over and the parents took what of their children's belongings they were allowed to have back...there might still be a few useful things lying around."

A few useful things...and a few dangerous things.

Just because she wasn't going to fall through the floor, that didn't mean Dawn didn't have to watch her step. It was entirely possible there were loose nails along with the crumbling bricks, or that one of the rats might make another appearance and not be quite so skittish.

Dawn, after all, was skittish enough on her own. The dark hallway lined with offices loomed before her, the ceilings so tall that she felt like a child just to be there. It seemed as if the hallway beckoned her down its path; wished to swallow her. She pushed her imagination away and focused on trying a few doors.

It was true—the building had been left mostly as-is at the time of its abandonment. Dawn couldn't blame them for leaving it this way, but it was eerie to open a door and find a desk, a file cabinet, a retro television. No radio, though.

She shut the door and tried another room. This one was some kind of medical ward, it seemed. Outdated medical equipment lay scattered and rusted around the room, and a cot in the corner rested crookedly behind a screen. Dawn had just slid open an empty drawer when a noise—the slamming of a door, she thought—echoed down the hall.

From the direction opposite the dining hall.

Her blood running cold, Dawn lifted her head from her investigation and edged into the dark corridor.

No other sounds emanated around the corner. She leaned around it, the lighter in hand, and struggled to stare through the darkness.

No movement distinguished itself from the empty space of the hallway.

Quiet as she could, Dawn edged toward the noise and wondered what it was. Maybe somebody really was staying there? If so, they'd better offer that person a beer or something—just to be friendly, and stave off trouble.

After determining that the courtyard door, nailed shut with several boards, was probably not the source of the noise, Dawn continued around another corner and found a hall not unlike the one on the way to the dining hall.

These large doors were closed. Dawn edged toward them while making as few sounds as possible. The lighter's flame danced in her hand with every movement. The handle of the door before her turned under the gentlest touch.

On the other side, Dawn found the chapel.

Though it was as dusty and dark as the other rooms, Dawn lingered in the doorway not due to fright, but due to the beauty of it. The chapel's design was old-fashioned somehow, with thick green carpet and a swirling pattern reminiscent of paisley on the walls, but the small room was nonetheless rich with an eerily pleasing aesthetic.

Somehow, it still looked prepared to host its next service. A crucifix up near the altar solemnly overlooked the pews; she was just edging toward it, lifting her lighter to see the carving more closely, when the Zippo illuminated something else.

A little clown doll smiled at her from the corner of a pew.

3.

EXPECTING THE PEWS to be empty as she had, Dawn's heart raced at the unexpected toy leering in the light of the Zippo. While she pressed a hand to her pounding chest, she bent down and investigated the strange toy.

What was a thing like this doing here? It did seem fairly old, she supposed...but, given that everything else in the neglected building seemed to belong more or less where it was, the clown doll was incredibly out-of-place.

Not to mention, free of dust.

Dawn had expected an allergy-inducing mushroom cloud to puff up when she lifted the toy from where it sat—yet, it seemed clean. Old, but clean.

The threadbare toy sported over-sized trousers decorated with polka dots. A colorful bow tie flopped down over the front of its shirt. With its red yarn hair and crooked beret, it could have been cute...were it not for the strange face, its arching eyebrows high over somehow lascivious eyes reminiscent of the curve of a too-long smile that was ornamented by buck teeth. Its patterned yellow shirt reminded Dawn somehow of the walls of the chapel around her. Its bottom was marked, in a child's scrawl, *Bongo*.

She shuddered, looking around as though someone might watch her.

The only one who did, it seemed, was the doll.

Shaking her head, Dawn set the doll down. As she did, an open cabinet caught her eye on the other side of the pew. Gasping, she hurried over to see its contents.

Candles!

With a relieved roll of her eyes and quick praise for somebody she only believed in when convenient, Dawn took a tall, green votive candle from the location of many more. After a certain point, she'd been more concerned about running out of lighter fluid than about finding music or light for the party. Bearing her new candle with her hand cupped around it, Dawn looked for something to help her transport the unlit candles back to her friends.

A basket sat among the debris at the base of the crucifix. The real miracle here was that the stained glass windows on either side of the cross were both still in perfect condition. They made her wonder how much of the mess in the room was made because of people breaking in, and how much was from the original cops carelessly investigating.

A shame the building had no caretaker. It was really a beautiful chapel.

Would have been, anyway, without all the litter, bits of crumbled plaster, and old pamphlets strewn about.

With a basket full of candles looped over her arm and the lit one flickering in her hand with each step she took, Dawn turned to exit the chapel—but there was Bongo, siting alone on the pew.

For some reason, she felt a little bad.

"I guess I owe you one for all this, huh, pal?" She shook the basket to demonstrate the candles and then, chuckling to herself, said, "All right...come on."

So, with Bongo, a collection of candles, and just a little bit of Barb's optimism growing in her heart, Dawn exited the chapel and made her way down the dark hall.

It only occurred to her once she'd left the chapel that she still had not determined the source of the noise that led her there in the first place. Though it was probably just some raccoon—or, heck, maybe another rat—she couldn't help but find herself hyper-vigilant.

Part of that was natural, of course. They were far from town and, with the weather the way that it was, if something went wrong they wouldn't be able to get help without a great deal of trouble and further risk. Therefore, her animal brain was wired to be ready for anything at any moment.

But the persistent nag in the back of Dawn's head kept her feeling like something else was wrong.

She just wasn't quite sure what it was.

Maybe it was the atmosphere. Goosebumps crawled up her arms as she navigated the dark hallways of the boarding school. Outside, wind howled. The occasional clap of thunder rattled the building upon its foundations. Some exterior windows had not been as lucky as the stained glass ones, and Dawn noticed through this or that sometimes open (sometimes missing) door that a few of the exposed rooms received a beating in the storm.

Would this mess ever let up? Maybe by morning...

Back in the dining hall, the chatting teenagers were interrupted by Dawn's call.

"Hey," she said into the room, not wanting to startle them. She still managed to surprise at least Mary, who was always a bit jumpy, and went on in apologetic tone, "I found candles, you guys!"

Barbara clapped her hands with delight. She rushed over to see the contents of the basket. "Yay, Dawn! Thank you! Oh, these are totally perfect—well! What's this fella doing here?"

"I found him in a pew," Dawn said with a laugh, drawing the clown from the basket and giving him a wave.

Barbie took him in her hands to laugh at his floppy arms and red yarn hair, clearly not quite as taken aback by his features as Dawn had been. The music student continued, "Looks like his name's Bongo. Kind of weird, huh?"

"I don't know, it's not so weird...kids probably bring all kinds of things from home when they're sent to a place like this."

Dawn didn't have a chance to point out that he hadn't been dusty when she discovered him. The other teenagers were already crowding around Dawn and Barb, enthusiastically deriding the doll for its perceived creepiness.

Kevin, in particular, seemed horrified. "What's with its face?"

"He'd probably ask you the same thing," Barb bandied back. While the girls tittered and Kevin rolled his eyes, Barbara hurried over to set Bongo upright beside the cooler of beer. "There! He can be our bartender."

Andrea laughed, saying, "There's something so innocent about you, Barbie."

"Well? He's got a bow tie and everything."

"Even better," Scott agreed with a laugh, lifting his already opened beer toward the toy, "we don't have to tip him."

Kevin chuckled in agreement while his friends, candles in-hand, lit them all from the flame flickering atop Dawn's. Gradually, the amount of light grew to something comfortable—even romantic.

The atmosphere changed in an instant. Smiles of relief plastered themselves to every face as, corner by corner, the room received just a little bit of life.

"You guys should come check out the chapel," Dawn said, sipping from her beer while Chris placed the final candle upon a cabinet near the entrance of the room. "It's in the other wing, super cool...kind of spooky, too."

"This whole *place* is spooky," Mary protested, wrapping her arms around herself and glancing about. "Ugh! How did you convince us to come here, again?"

"It would have been more fun and felt safer if there had been more people," Dawn said with a shrug, leaping to Barb's defense before the girl needed to defend herself. "Still, it's a dry place to wait out the storm until morning."

"Yeah," said Barb, nodding. "And it's a cool experience! To be honest, though..."

Her eyes lowering, Barbara laughed in a weak way and rubbed her hand over her forehead. "I'm super embarrassed! I had all these grand aspirations for what tonight was going to be like. Now we don't even have music."

"We could make our own music," said Dawn, leaning forward upon the box where she sat. "Or—oh!"

It was all the candles around that did it. Grinning, her increase in confidence after venturing into the dark of the school inspiring her to tease her friends, she suggested, "Why don't we try to do a séance?"

A few glances were shared among the students. Andrea asked, "A séance? For, like, the victims of the massacre or whatever?"

"Sure! Or—Barb's aunt. That's how it always works in stories, right? You need a personal connection to the ghosts you're summoning, or something. It probably helps, anyway."

But Mary was already shaking her head rapidly, her red curls flying back and forth and significantly frizzier after having been exposed to the rain.

"No way," she said, her voice firm. "I'm not messing around with that stuff."

Nudging her with an elbow, Scott mockingly asked, "You don't really believe in this stuff, do you? It's just fooling. All in your head, you know."

"I've heard lots of stories about people who think it's all in their head before something horrible happens! The last thing I want to do is see—I don't know, a walking shadow, or for me to look in a mirror and discover my reflection's not my own."

"Ah, come on—"

"No, Scott!" Her tone increasing somewhat in pitch, Mary insisted, "This place is already freaky enough without a *séance!* This whole time, I've felt like I'm being watched."

Shuddering, tightening her arms around herself, Mary shook her head. "I know I sound stupid and superstitious," she summarized. "But that stuff just doesn't seem fun to me."

Just like that, Dawn felt bad for even suggesting such a goofy thing. Nonetheless, Scott seemed ready to rib his girlfriend. "Ah, come on. You can't really believe something's going to happen! You don't believe in ghosts, do you?"

While Mary stewed sullenly, her boyfriend ignored all the STOP signs and blazed right along.

"If you feel like you're being watched," Scott continued, "maybe it's Bongo over there making you feel that way. Are you afraid of clowns, too?"

Scowling, Mary jerked her arm away from his next nudge. "*Stop* it, Scott."

"Yeah, Scott," advised Andrea, "take it easy on the teasing, would you? It's normal to be freaked out by a place like this."

"Yeah, but by the idea of doing a séance? I didn't know you were so—" For lack of a specific term, he wiggled his fingers and settled on, "Mystical."

"I just have respect for things that other people don't," said Mary, snatching her boyfriend's beer from his hand and chugging the remaining contents while he complained. After she tipped her head forward again and took a little breath while wiping suds from her lips, she went on.

"You know—maybe it *is* that doll freaking me out.

I've felt worse ever since it came into the room."

"Oh," said Scott dryly while she strode over to pluck Bongo from his seat, "so now you're psychic, or something?"

"No, jerk! What's wrong with you?" Shaking her head, looking like she was trying to remember what it was that got her in this relationship in the first place, Mary looked reluctantly into the face of the doll. She grimaced. "Who would give this kind of toy to a kid? It's so creepy..."

"All toys used to be a little creepy," said Dawn. "Have you ever seen old Halloween costumes from the 1920s? Way scarier than they are now!"

With a theatrical shudder, Mary turned toward the doorway with the doll in her hand—

And dropped it as she screamed.

Those that were seated leapt upright; those already standing jolted in surprise. All eyes turned fearfully toward the doorway.

A figure stood in the darkness of the open frame.

4.

THE MIDDLE-AGED WOMAN at the dining hall's entrance seemed to be in a kind of stupor. She regarded the teenagers through tired eyes while they recovered from their scare, couples having jolted together and hands having pressed to staggered hearts until the figure resolved into this: a despondent woman.

"Not here," she whispered as though to herself, her gray gaze sweeping past their faces as if none of them existed at all. "She's not here."

Chris's hold on Andrea had begun to relax. The jock's brow furrowed while she glanced at her boyfriend, then asked this stranger, "Are you all right, ma'am?"

The stranger's bitter little laugh sounded more like a cough than anything close to mirth.

"You know what, no—I'm not." Rubbing the bridge of her nose, her eyes squeezing shut, she spoke as if she at last remembered to be an adult when she said somewhat weakly, "You kids shouldn't be here."

"Hey, man"—Scott, always on the defensive—"we're not kids. We just graduated."

"It's dangerous up here," the woman insisted. "It's incredibly dangerous. This is a bad place."

Waving his beer, the pockmarked under-achiever asked, "Then why are you here?"

She stared at Scott hard in return. "Because I'm looking for Janie. My little Janie, I came to pick her up, and—have you seen her?"

The mood in the room was at once all the more tense. While the teenagers glanced at one another, Barbara, stepped forward and asked, "We haven't, no. How old is she?"

"Only nine," whispered the lady. One hand pressed to her cheek, then slid up to push long, thin strands of dark brown hair back from her sunken eyes. "Janie is nine."

"What's a nine-year-old kid doing in a place like this?" Chris couldn't help but scoff at her a bit. He shook his head. "You're not making any sense, lady."

"You're right. Kids shouldn't play in places like these. You shouldn't, either—Bongo!"

The woman's eyes widened to see the doll lying on the floor near Mary. Her motions were quick and somehow feral. She lurched upon it, desperate as though for the safety and comfort of a friend.

"Oh, Bongo! This is my Janie's. Where did you find him?"

"In the chapel," Dawn answered. "Sitting at the end of a pew."

40

As soon as her hands made contact with the little clown doll, the woman's eyes overflowed with tears. Her façade collapsed into an expression of grief so terrible it made Dawn afraid to be a mother, lest she ever experience its like.

"Oh, Janie!"

Eyes shut, the woman pressed the doll to her forehead. She rocked unnervingly, weeping while the teenagers responded with varying levels of discomfort. Chris and Kevin exchanged the sort of look that silently declared the woman to be unhinged; Scott edged away. Andrea, frozen, looked like she was hoping the conversation would be over soon.

Mary just said, "I told you guys. This place is bad news."

"We haven't seen anybody," said Barbara, empathetic as she always was. "And we definitely haven't seen a little kid. But we'll keep an eye out and let you know if we run into her."

"Thank you," said the woman. "Thank you so much."

"It's no trouble, Mrs..."

"McDonnell," answered the woman, rising to her feet with Barbara's firm guidance. While thunder roared on outside, Mrs. McDonnell found her footing and smiled bravely through her tears.

"You'll all so very kind," she said, adding firmly, "but you shouldn't stay here."

"We're sort of stuck until the storm clears," Kevin told her with a nod in the direction of the rattling wall. "So, as much as we'd like to leave, we just have to make the best of things for right now...serves us right for not turning back when we had the chance, I guess."

"I guess," parroted the woman, studying him for a

41

prolonged period of time before turning away.

Alone, without a light, Mrs. McDonnell shambled off into the darkness.

The teenagers looked at each other when her back was turned, but everyone waited until she was all the way down the hall before making any move. Kevin strode over and shut the dining hall doors, then paused in front of them with a grim expression.

"That was weird," he understated, shaking his head. "I hope she finds her daughter. You didn't see anything other than that doll, did you, Dawn?"

"I would have said something if I had," she said, looking with concern at the doorway. "Wonder what the kid was doing up here in the first place?"

"Probably brought her up here herself and lost track of her," proposed Chris with a shake of his head. "She seemed a little bit—you know. Not all there, as Mom says."

"Shut up!" Dawn plucked her beer from the top of the covered desk she'd last set it on, then leaned back against the very same. "If you couldn't find your kid, you'd probably seem a little out of it, too."

The jarring clang that echoed through the dining hall as Dawn perched against the desk surprised at least Mary. Dawn's breath, however, hitched in a soft gasp of excitement. Her frown fell away.

"A piano," she declared, turning to pull the cover from the instrument that had been rolled into storage alongside so many cedar crates and molding cardboard boxes. While Andrea and Scott made noises of relief, and Barbie put her worries aside to come and check it out, Mary hung back by the spot where the doll had fallen from her hand.

"You okay, Mary?"

Kevin's question was soft; audible only to Mary and the room in which they stood. Especially once Dawn sat down and began plinking at the piano to determine if it was playable. Frowning, Mary shook her head.

"This night just keeps getting worse and worse. I don't know—I don't think we should have come here. Are you really sure your Jeep can't get back down the mountain?"

"We were lucky to make it all the way here, honestly. I think once it lets up a little we should have a good chance of getting back down, but...I don't know. I just feel like I'd rather wait until it's light outside, you know?"

Scott called over to his girlfriend and demanded, "Quit being such a wet blanket, Mary! We're here. Let's just have a good time—what are you worried about that crazy lady for?"

"She's not crazy," Mary insisted. "At least, she didn't seem crazy to me. I just don't like the thought of hanging out like everything's normal when a kid is lost somewhere in this building."

"I'm sure Mrs. McDonnell will find her daughter eventually," consoled Kevin.

Mary, visibly skeptical, shook her head.

"If something happens to a child in this place while we're just hanging around, and we could have done something to intervene—I don't think I'll be able to live with myself."

Sighing, rolling his eyes, Scott took a swig of his second beer and told her, "You're so dramatic. Getting all high and mighty about some kid...acting scared of séances...say, maybe that McDonnell lady isn't alive at all!"

Mary's fists balled at her sides. "Stop it, Scott," she demanded right in front of everyone. "Stop it, don't even talk about it."

But, laughing like a cruel boy on the playground, Scott went on bullying the girl that he liked. "Yeah— maybe she's a ghost. If we bump into her daughter, *she'll* turn out to be a ghost, too!"

"Stop it, stop it—I'm so sick of this, Scott. You always take things too far! You never listen to what I want or treat me with any respect."

"Because! You're being childish. You need to grow up, Mary."

The room somehow felt even more painfully awkward during the argument than when Mrs. McDonnell had been weeping on the floor. Everybody else avoided eye contact while the two of them went at it, going through the pre-break up rituals so many couples were doomed to endure before parting ways for college.

"*I* need to grow up!" Mary stared at her boyfriend, incredulous, her hand to her sternum. *"Me? You should try listening to yourself some time! I can't help it that this place gives me the creeps, and here you are—making it worse!"*

"There's nothing to be scared of out there! Look, you want me to prove it?"

Setting his beer atop the piano that Dawn played to give the rest of the room something to focus on outside of the conflict, Scott launched himself from the spot where he leaned. He took up a blue candle on his way to the door, saying to Mary, "I'll show you."

"Scott," she began—

Too late.

The dining hall door shut behind Scott. Bristling,

Mary remained where she stood.

One question seemed to float through the heads of everyone still in the room: Should someone go after him?

The tension in the air thickened. Now awkwardness faded into fear. Say something did go wrong out there, in the dark of the hallway?

"See"—Scott's voice rang merrily through the door from about halfway to the unexplored set of stairs—"there's nothing to be afraid—hey."

His tone took a sudden shift when he cut himself off. Mary rolled her eyes, already visibly angry to be toyed with.

"That is *not* funny, Scott," she told him, her shoe stomping lightly upon the hard floor. "I don't know why you always dig yourself deeper."

But Scott didn't respond.

At least, not to Mary.

"Who's there?"

His voice was edged with panic and the teenagers exchanged an urgent look.

Mary rolled her angrily watering eyes, hands on the hips of her white polka-dotted dress. "He's just trying to mess with—"

"Stop that. Stop!" Mary's face fell and she took a step forward, freezing again only when Chris held out a hand. Scott yelled on, "Don't come any closer! No!"

Kevin looked urgently around for something he could use as a weapon. In the end he only found an empty beer bottle in his immediate vicinity. With it held like a bludgeon, he approached the door just as Scott's voice erupted in a terrible, high-pitched scream. Mary screamed, too.

Tensed for action, Kevin threw open the door.

"Gotcha!"

Scott howled with laughter where he stood midway down the hall, the candle in his hand illuminating the juvenile mirth of his face.

All the fear in Mary's expression transformed to rage at once. Her teeth bared in her fury. Saying absolutely nothing, she strode out of the dining hall and toward her unpleasant boyfriend. Still he laughed, on and on, until Mary came to a stop before him.

"I can't believe you guys fell for that! You really are a bunch of—hey!"

Having snatched the candle from his hand, Mary marched down the hall and warned through angry tears, "Don't follow me."

"Now wait, Mary! Hold on, come back—"

"Let her go, Scott," said Andrea firmly. "She's right. You've been acting like a jerk. Give her a few minutes to herself before you start into her again."

"Ah, come on. You're going to go walking into the darkness when you're so afraid in the light? Mary? Mary!"

His echo succumbed to silence.

5.

MARY WAS JUST so mad that suddenly she wasn't afraid of the darkness at all. Mary wasn't afraid of a thing, in fact, except for how angry Scott made her.

The truth was that he was always like this. She just managed to rationalize his behavior when they were alone, or in a situation that bothered her less. But now, in a place where she felt unsafe, he failed worse than ever to step up to the plate.

How had she managed to lie to herself all this time? Maybe it was just for the sake of having a boyfriend— of looking cool and fitting in. Oh, at one point in time Scott had been very charming and sweet. Then he had gotten comfortable. Once people got comfortable in a relationship and they were no longer on their best behavior, well—sometimes what one thought they'd had and what one actually had proved to be two different things.

At the juncture in the corridor, Mary took a left. Thankfully, Scott didn't follow her. He let her go without more than a derisive wave of his hand before he turned back to enter the dining hall. She went on, making her way down the hallway and its many offices, shut and open.

It seemed like more doors were open now than before. Dawn, probably. Mary tried not to be unnerved by it. She should have asked Dawn for clearer directions to the chapel she'd found, but oh! Mary was just so mad.

When she got frustrated like that, it was hard to think of practical things like directions. Add on top of that the personal insult, and Mary was lucky she'd stopped to snatch away Scott's candle.

It was disturbing to her that her own boyfriend should treat her this way. What was annoying or sometimes even slightly upsetting teasing back in town was, when she felt imperiled, a sign of how lightly he took her opinion—and how flippantly he regarded her personal safety.

Who wanted a boyfriend like that?

Moreover...what was really the point of staying together when they were eighteen, about to go to different colleges in different cities? Wasn't it a little unrealistic to try to pull off some sort of long-distance thing?

There was so much to see and do in the world. There were many people more mature than Scott. There was too much life left in Mary to think of living the rest of it with Scott.

Her heart and mind becoming unified on a decision that had been in the making since the two had gotten together, Mary wandered down the hall and tried a few of the doors. Nothing very exciting, it seemed. She wandered around the corner and paused near a boarded door that, based on the raging of the storm on the other side, must have led to a courtyard. Mary wondered what shape it was in now. Awful, no doubt.

The storm howled around her. She continued through the hall, her candle's flickering light softly illuminating the haggard faces of many a martyr depicted in the paintings on the walls. Mary averted her eyes from these, unwilling to worsen her own mood.

Not that there was any better place to look in the eerie school, anyway. In this eastern wing of the building, Mary found a bathroom and a shower room. They reminded her of the ones in the dormitory of the college she had settled on...only much more decrepit, and much more frightening. The stalls of the reddish shower room were missing their curtains. Its uncanny feeling had more in common with a meatpacking plant than it did with a bathroom.

Shuddering, Mary emerged from the shower room and looked around.

The feeling of being watched was getting stronger. She never would have talked about it because of people like Scott—people who would make fun of her. But, sometimes, Mary swore she could feel...energy, maybe. Or intention.

How could she describe it? It was like feeling static in her brain, or a subtle warping of reality. She had never seen anything like a ghost, but she had sometimes felt presences. Felt the sensation of intense focus upon her, eyes on her, without really knowing where it was coming from or what it was all about.

She felt that now, in the halls of St. Cecilia's Preparatory School, stronger than ever before.

Just confronting herself with that notion made her anger fade and her skin crawl. Fear slowly rising up her spinal column to chill the back of her skull once again, Mary decided that the chapel wasn't that important to clearing her mind after all.

Her destination unreached, she turned around to go back to the dining hall. As she turned each corner, her steps got just a little faster. That strange, warping feeling became all the more urgent.

Mary had just passed the office with the pane of frosted glass when the nun peeled out of the darkness behind her, knife flashing through the air like a bright blue moonbeam.

When the blade lifted again, that same cloaking darkness left it purple-black with the red of Mary's blood.

As Mary screamed, the nun screamed along with her—a hideous, almost inhuman scream that filled the teenager's ears and tested the upper limits of her heart rate.

Pain blazed all down her arm. Unable to comprehend what was truly happening, Mary threw the candle at her assailant and sprinted into the darkness.

The nun wailed like a banshee as it pursued its prey, this monstrous shrieking coming in waves like a dog gasping for breath between barks. It moved with a speed that would have been too much for even athletic Andrea. The knife stabbed down through the air just behind Mary more than once, its fearful wails nearly in her ear.

Mary urged herself to run a little faster.

Gasping for air, she screamed, "Help! Oh, God! Please, somebody help me," in a tone higher and more urgent than she'd ever known herself capable of producing.

The nun unleashed a sound like a horrible moan. Whether the moan of a ghost or a killer kept for ages in a padded cell, Mary wasn't sure.

Whatever it was, she couldn't lead it to her friends. She had to lead it somewhere else and find a place to hide.

Up the stairs. Maybe she could find a dormitory with a closet, or a bathroom with some stalls, or—

Mary's thoughts vanished into a miasma of surprise, fear, and the anticipation of pain. She had mounted the stairs to the second floor and sped up them two at a time—but the landing her foot had expected was not there.

Instead, Mary dropped into a pit full of razor wire.

Mary careened into it with an echoing scream—a noise prolonged by the hot agony of razors slicing into her flesh and hooking her there for the predator in pursuit. She twisted and thrashed in the sea of coils, each twist and push she made to clamber out serving to embed her more deeply among the hateful metal thorns.

Her screams reaching a fever pitch, Mary sobbed Scott's name and squirmed toward the open doorway perhaps two feet above her head.

Oh, God! If she could just reach it, she could pull herself out. Her forearm slit open along the coil of razors entangling it as she reached toward the staircase. Tears rushing out of her eyes and down her cheeks, she fought against the sting and forced herself to go limp. If she kept struggling, she was going to kill herself for sure. But if she could calmly, slowly stretch her arm up...

The whispering started when her fingertips were two inches or so from the lip of the stairs.

With a wretched sob, Mary cried the word, "No," and recoiled into the baleful embrace of the razor wires. They took her gleefully, drawing bright red lines along her calves and thighs and slipping across her cheek to sever the tissue.

As the rapidly whispering nun's black veil slid into view, Mary could hardly feel the razors. Her heart hammered in her ears, blotting out the whispering.

The uselessness of screaming left her mute as the nun's long arm extended into the pit. Its black gloved fingers sank into Mary's mane of glorious red curls and yanked her halfway out of the razor wires, jerking back her head to expose her throat.

Mary's eyes widened with the terrible reality of the situation.

The nun's knife slit open the flesh of her throat.

Hot blood spilled over Mary's dress to stain its white spots the same bright red as the rest of it.

While Mary produced a few final shocked gurgles, the nun shoved her face-first into the pit.

Her steadily dripping blood would rust those wires forever.

6.

THE WHOLE SCENE really soured after Mary left the party, Dawn couldn't help but notice. People were appreciative of her music and glad for the beer, but nobody seemed to know what to say.

Especially not to Scott. He sat sullenly by the dining hall door, waiting for Mary to come back through any moment. To his credit, he didn't drink; then again, he didn't do anything. Rather than save face by continuing to try to have a good time with his friends, he had fallen into a sulk. Now the rest of them had to suffer for it.

"Maybe we should play some sort of game," Barbara suggested. "We could do some kind of scavenger hunt, or maybe a—"

"Would you cut it out, Barbara?" Scott leaned back upon the box where he sat, staring at the ceiling and the roaring deluge. "The party is ruined, okay? I know it's your urge to make everything perfect and be a good little hostess, but you can't fix this. We're stuck on a mountain in the middle of a storm, my girlfriend is going to break up with me, who knows if we're even going to make it back tomorrow—and, let's face it! Only one of those is my fault."

Her face darkening with shame, Barbara glanced away and said, "I feel just awful. I know I take things lightly sometimes. I just—"

The first scream pierced through the twisting architecture of the school.

"Very funny," said Scott sourly to the door. He raised his voice. "And very mature, might I add, for somebody who just called me childish!"

"Help! Oh, God! Please, somebody help me!"

Dawn had stopped playing at the first scream. This one chilled her to the bone.

She looked urgently into the faces of her friends around. Each one of them was frozen with uncertainty. No doubt, each thought the same thing: that Mary could occasionally be a bit immature, just like Scott. But something like this just didn't seem like her.

Especially not when she was so angry. She was the type to blow up and scream in somebody's face in front of other people. Unhealthy, but direct and to-the-point. Passive aggressively trying to prove some point to Scott just didn't seem like her.

"I think she might really be in trouble," Kevin said, the bottle still in his hand. "Listen to her!"

Another awful set of screams rose up from the end of the hall. The teenagers held their collective breath.

Dawn had never heard a scream so awful in all her life. She sprang from the piano and stood near Barbara, who for her own part looked totally overwhelmed by conflicting urges. Even Andrea, who was normally about as dynamic and can-do as Kevin, recoiled toward Chris.

Scott paled.

"She's just trying to get one over on me," he nonetheless insisted, arms crossed. "I'm sure she's fine. What could be happening?"

"Maybe she found that kid and something's wrong," Kevin said quickly, stepping toward the doors. "Or maybe she's been hurt. We should check, in any case."

"Ah, come on. We'll go out there and—"

One more high scream, bright as a bolt of lightning—cut off mid-execution.

His face filling with genuine fright, Scott at last sprang upright. "Mary," he cried, darting through the door with bravery the frightened teenagers all sensed to be too little, too late.

Kevin rushed over and shut the dining hall's main entrance behind Scott. Then, still with his hand upon the surface of the door, he turned to face his remaining friends.

"I think we'd ought to risk the road back down the mountain," he said to Barbara, who had begun to nod rapidly even before he went on. "Don't you?"

She might have answered if Scott's scream—a true scream, no jest in it but only mortal terror—hadn't echoed down the hallway.

Another scream. The hefty sound of running footsteps.

Footsteps coming closer.

Kevin, his face lined with urgent panic and the former boy scout's eternal willingness to help, threw open the right door of the dining hall.

"What happened, Sco—"

The nun glided into view knife-first, this bloody blade arcing down and into Kevin's chest.

His features widened in an expression of shock— shock, and terrible comprehension.

By the time the knife jerked back out of his torso, the women and Chris were all screaming.

Kevin dropped the bottle and lurched back a few steps. Barbara screamed his name: devastated, frightened, traumatized.

The nun lunged upon him, grabbing his reddening shirt with one hand and using the other to stab hole after hole into his wholesome, all-American flesh.

Lifting his hands to absorb a few stabs, Kevin produced a gagging sound and spat out a mouthful of blood.

The room dissolved into absolute chaos.

Dawn's head whipped wildly around at motion in the corner of her eye. She looked just in time to watch Chris sprint out of the dining hall's secondary entrance without waiting for Andrea or trying to drag her along. In fact, Andrea herself only noticed he was gone after a few seconds.

Gritting her teeth, the volleyball player dashed after her cowardly boyfriend.

Dawn considered following them, but the nun seemed attracted by their fast movements. Black veil jerking up in the direction of the running teenagers, its eyes and cheekbones cloaked in terrible shadows from the dim candlelight around the room, the nun dashed after them and left Dawn and Barbara where they were—huddled together at the piano along the edge of the room.

While the killer whisked after Chris and Andrea,

Dawn made for the primary exit of the dining hall. She stopped when she realized Barb didn't follow her.

"Come on, Barbie!" Dawn caught her friend's hand and looked urgently into her face. "We have to get out of here."

"Kevin," whispered Barbara, her pupils microscopic with horror as she stared at her boyfriend's body. "Kevin, Kevin—"

He was totally still, flat on his back in a puddle of his own fluids. His face appeared still contorted in shock, but the nun's blade had entered his heart, his throat, and his lungs. Sometimes he made a wretched little gurgling noise. The gurgling then became a clicking sound, a hard 'K' sound produced again and again as though he tried to say his own name.

Barbara hurried to her boyfriend's side and tearfully took his body in her arms. He winced sharply, wheezing with pain, barely able to move his arms the agony was so great. Still, one hand managed to move an inch or two in the direction of his trouser pocket.

"K," he continued. "K—k—k—keys."

"Your car keys," Barbara said, gasping, tears rolling down her cheeks even as she hurriedly searched his pockets. "Oh, yes, of course, yes—Kevin! Oh, Kevin. I love you. It'll be okay, Kevin—"

"No. Go," he whispered. "Go, go. I'm dead."

Blood flooded across Barbie's hands and splattered over her dress. Gritting her teeth, clearly struggling to see through the tears, Barbara reached into Kevin's pocket and took the keys.

Dawn, meanwhile, hovered nervously just outside the doorway of the room.

"Come on, Barbara, hurry! We have to get out of here."

Nodding, chin warping with her sorrow, Barbara slid her boyfriend back down into his blood. "We'll find somewhere to call for help," she told him, offering the coldest comfort there was.

Kevin said nothing, his head sagging back upon the floor.

What an awful sight! Dawn could hardly endure it. Simply seeing him there on the ground burned her limbs with terrible sympathy pains.

What was it like to be stabbed that way?

Maybe she shouldn't wonder too hard, lest she find out.

"Come on," Dawn said, rushing down the darkened hall, "this way."

With one more tearful glance back at her dying boyfriend, Barbie succumbed to the urgency of the situation and dashed after Dawn. The music student led the way back down the hall and around the corner, her memory of the way they'd first come fairly hazy compared to her more recent tour of the school. It was a twisting building and she wasn't sure she could quickly find the staircase that had let them into this floor.

Therefore, after charging down the dark hall of offices, Dawn took a gamble. She led Barb left, toward the sealed courtyard, and at that door went right instead of forward. Another series of rooms was arranged on either side of this hall—classrooms, it seemed—but at the end of the imposing building was a broad foyer.

Above the storm, a crackling noise filled Dawn's heart with fear.

Surely she was hearing things.

Surely that was not the sound of a raging fire.

The front entrance to the school proved just as immobile from inside as from outside. While Barbara, trembling with fear and covered in her boyfriend's blood, skidded to a halt, Dawn looked around. A few bricks had come free from the masonry and lay in a clutter nearby one of the classrooms. Dawn had just snatched one up when Barbara's head whipped in the direction of a door's distant *slam.*

"What's going on?" Barb whispered the words, rushing up to try the same handle that Dawn had just shaken right in front of her. "Oh, God, it's not working—it's not working!"

Barbie rattled it all the more wildly while, with an empathetic glance at her friend, Dawn ran into the adjacent classroom and threw the brick straight through a window. Its seal long-since broken and its glass rendered opaque by dirt, the window seemed happy enough to yield to the brick's demands.

Its absence revealed a scene that made Dawn feel as though she were about to throw up.

In defiance of the storm that rattled the school, a terrible fire had consumed the Jeep and now raged around the metal skeleton of its frame.

Frightened to be left alone for even a second, Barbara bolted into the classroom where Dawn stood in a daze. "Dawn? What was that? What's that smell?"

Dawn found she couldn't reply. She looked helplessly up at Barbara, who then belatedly peered out the window.

The expression on Barbara's face was not one of shock. Not quite. It was a kind of hollowing. As if, seeing their primary means of escape destroyed before their eyes, whatever fundamental life essence it was that made Barbara 'Barbara' withered up within the shell of her external body. Her lips parted, but no sound came out. Her eyes widened, and her pupils looked smaller than ever.

Her body shook so violently that her teeth chattered.

When at last she managed to form words, they were punctuated by a terrible dental clacking. "What are we going to do, Dawn?"

"I don't know," whispered Dawn, looking helplessly up at Barbara. "I don't know. Maybe—what if you walked down the mountain and got help?"

"I can't." Eyes filling with new tears, Barbara looked toward the tempest and said, "It's so dark, I don't think I can make it. I can't tell where I'm going if I'm just walking in rain like this."

"Well, one of us has to get down there and get help."

Dawn thought about volunteering, but immediately realized she couldn't leave Barbara alone in this terrible place. How would she be able to live with herself if she let her friend stay behind to die? There was Chris and Andrea to think about, too, let alone the whereabouts of Scott and Mary. And, well...

Barbara was right. In the dark and driving rain, it would be impossible to see erosion in the road—whether it was that very same that initially stopped them, or a new section that had gone out since they'd made it to the top of the mountain. Trying to walk down the road was best saved for the abatement of the storm, if not the morning light.

But was it really any more dangerous than staying on the premises of St. Cecilia's?

Dawn had no chance to ponder this before the nun's rapid steps echoed down the hall.

1.

WITH THE NUN rushing straight toward them, Dawn flew into survival mode again. Paying little mind to her own security, the music student knocked a few more shards of glass from the window frame and pushed Barbara toward it.

"Hide outside somewhere," she urged her friend. "If you can't get down the mountain, at least hide someplace safe up here. I'll call to you when—whenever I can."

"I don't want to be alone, Dawn, please!"

"Go! Go, Barbara. I don't want to watch you die the way you had to watch Kevin!"

With an odd sort of look at that, Barbara seemed poised to protest further—until, at the sound of their whispering, the footsteps paused in apparent thought. Only then did Barbie let Dawn help her out the window. She vaulted over the edge and landed five feet down. Dawn was thinking that she might also boost herself up, but that would have taken too long.

And the nun delayed for nothing.

Somehow Dawn had expected the nun to behave normally. The normal thing to do, when one entered a room and found a person in it, was to pause and assess that person. The nun, however, did not behave like a person.

It behaved like a spider, scuttling out of trapdoor holes and snatching hapless prey.

The shudder-inducing image rushed through Dawn's head while the nun, without pausing for a second, swept into the room. The knife gleamed, still red with Kevin's blood, ready and eager to pierce more human flesh. With a reflexive scream, Dawn scrambled around the overturned desks and even sprang over one when the quick-moving nun got a little too close. Landing, Dawn urged her limbs into double-time and broke out of the room with a cry of alarm.

All the while, the nun screamed after her—whether mocking her or echoing her like a dull animal, Dawn wasn't sure. Either way, it was the most chilling scream she had ever heard a human produce. She had to wonder if the nun even qualified for such a category.

Throwing the door shut behind her for a few seconds of added delay, Dawn dashed back up the hall and around the corner to the left.

There had to be another way out of this school. Another window that was easier to reach, or a back door, or that same side entrance. Then she could meet Barbara outside!

And then...then they could make their perilous descent together, thinking all the way of the people left behind. Andrea and Chris—and what about Scott and Mary? Had they met the same fate as Kevin?

Dawn's mind raced. All the while, her eyes whipped over the office doors lining the hall. Through an open door she passed, she glanced at one of those same broken windows she noticed earlier.

Her flight instinct may have been strong, but it couldn't justify abandoning her friends...and the shards of glass still clinging to the frame were not only thick, but big. Jumping through one without taking the time to clear it out would be suicide.

Gritting her teeth, resisting the temptation, Dawn continued running through the hall of offices. The storming footsteps of the nun beat a rapid pursuit. Could Dawn find a place to hide? Could she find a weapon to fight back?

The nurse's station. It was a gamble, but better than nothing.

Heart hammering, Dawn took a sharp left into the cramped little room. She slammed the door behind her and dove beneath the cot, grateful she could even fit. Shutting her eyes, Dawn wondered if praying was appropriate in this situation.

Outside, at the end of the hall, feet beat upon the alarming floorboards.

A door slammed open.

Dawn focused on maintaining her breathing.

The footsteps carried on, drawing closer.

Another slam.

Dawn kept her eyes shut and drew her limbs tighter under the squat little bed.

A new wave of footsteps.

Another slam, this so heavy and so nearby that the door to the infirmary rattled along with it.

Dawn filled her lungs and held her breath.

The footsteps next stopped outside her door.

As the knob turned, it protested weakly and only gave at the hard shove of the nun's shoulder.

Biting her lip, Dawn forced herself to look.

The killer stepped into the room, a shadow in its habit.

It lingered just within the boundary of the room. While it stood and looked around, Dawn's lungs began to burn. She shut her eyes again and waited, hoping that luck was with her.

One step into the room. Two.

Had the boys' cologne gotten on her while they were together in the Jeep?

Could her pursuer see the edge of her foot or some telltale shadow from her elbow?

Was Dawn's heart really as loud as it seemed to be, banging away in her ears?

The floorboards creaked beneath the nun's feet.

It wandered away to try the next room.

Dawn waited until she heard that door slam to release the breath she'd been holding. While gasping as quietly as she could for precious air, she let a few tears escape her long-resisting eyes. Briny sorrow mingled with relief and her mind raced to find a solution to this problem.

Before she found a reliable means of escape, the first thing Dawn had to do was check the status of each of her friends. She had to at least try to get them out with her. She had the sinking feeling that a few would be dead by the time she found them, but if that were the case, well...

At least they'd be accounted for.

Quietly focused on steadying her breath, Dawn lay beneath the cot and listened to the steps of the nun. It was impossible for the girl to tell how long she remained in hiding. Two minutes? Five? Twenty? It felt like an eternity was spent waiting for the nun's footsteps to fade around the corner.

When they finally did, Dawn remained where she was for a moment more. What was it her mother had told her when she was overwhelmed during the process of applying for schools?

Break a big task into lots of little ones, the chipper woman had said in a comforting tone. *Then just focus on getting those small tasks done one at a time!*

If only she were there!

Actually...if Dawn's mother were there, she would be in as much danger as the rest of them.

Still, it ached Dawn to think she might never see her own mother again. How would that affect not just her mother, but her father? They would have been crushed—raising their daughter to the age of eighteen, only to have her murdered by a psychopathic nun in an abandoned old boarding school. What a devastating fate that would have been for them all!

She couldn't let that happen. Dawn had to see her family again, whatever it took...but she had to be able to look them in the face, too.

Maybe, if she found a phone or a two-way radio, she would be able to contact someone for assistance and have them on the way while she rounded up her friends. She still wasn't sure about the power situation, but Kevin was probably right. Somewhere, there had to be a generator. If she could figure out how to turn it on and get the school power, a huge part of her problem would be solved.

That was a big 'if,' though. It didn't exactly thrill her to think of searching through this dark school and evading its killer nun for something that may or may not have been there...but Dawn didn't have a better option. All she could do was move quietly, pay attention, and try to waste no time in collecting her friends.

Quietly as she could, Dawn slid from beneath the cot and sat upright. As she did, something in her pocket cut into her leg. Frowning, she reached in and dug out the cool metal object.

Chris's Zippo felt oh so comforting in her hand.

Sighing, Dawn kissed the lighter and scrambled to her feet. The flame blazed up when she thrust back the lid. Though it provided a meager amount of illumination, it was certainly better than navigating in complete darkness. At least the area directly around her was clear, although more than a few feet away the hall outside the infirmary was as cloaked as the body of their assailant. All that mattered was her ability to search the rooms around.

One of these offices had to have some way of contacting the outside world. How did the teachers of the boarding school do it before the massacre, after all? She paused in the darkness, her eyes struggling to make out all the doors as she scanned up and down the hall.

Dawn didn't know a lot about the professional world, but at the age of eighteen, she knew plenty about schools. She knew that principals, headmistresses, and all other forms of school leadership liked to distinguish themselves from the rabble about as much as all other bosses in the world. Therefore, when her scrutinizing gaze landed on the office door with the glass panel, she heard it screaming, "Check me!"

From her last trip down the hall, however, she knew it was locked and didn't want to waste time by rattling the knob. If she was going to attract attention with a noise, it had might as well be a useful one.

Her gaze fell upon a rock that rested near her feet.

At this rate, Dawn was shaping up to be a first-rate delinquent! The office window required more force to break than the shabby one in the front of the school, owing perhaps to the thickness of the frosted glass. When at last it gave, however, it gave far more cleanly than had the exterior window that let Barb out. A good thing: the sound of the shattering glass was liable to attract attention, and Dawn felt a countdown timer ticking over her head.

Heart pounding, Dawn clambered through the window in the door and emerged in an office that was certainly comfortable enough to be the head mistress's. It felt as if she had broken into an untouched pharaoh's tomb. A few couches were strewn about, in surprisingly good condition after the passage of so many years—maybe because the office received no external light. Even the papers on the desk still seemed in order.

Even the sprays of blood, bright red long-since dried black, still decorated the sides of the desk and boards of the floor.

Shuddering, Dawn imagined she could see just where a body was once found sitting up against the furniture. She forced herself to look at the desk as an impartial object, rather than a crime scene accoutrement.

A powerful piece of oak furniture with claw feet

and a height designed to intimidate children, the desk seemed in largely untouched condition since the crime—though Dawn couldn't help but notice the folders scattered around at the floor, as if a file cabinet had been rummaged through. Did somebody have a key in here? More artifacts of police involvement?

Some kind of angry ghost?

Ugh! As if.

Ignoring the disordered files, Dawn briefly checked the desk's surface. No luck! No sign of a telephone. Removed during an investigation, maybe, or never there at all; Dawn wasn't sure. For good measure, knowing the school was very old, she checked along the walls, but there was no rotary dialer mounted to any of them.

She swept the lighter past bookshelves and religious paintings, an old grandfather clock, and another squat, heavy, old-fashioned television. Nothing that was of use to her, it seemed.

And no way out to escape the footsteps that honed in on her from the far side of the hall.

Panic surged through Dawn's body. She considered hiding behind the couch but knew that, if the nun should appear and get into the room with her, she would be trapped in the corner. Dawn would be a goner, for sure.

Were there any weapons? A paperweight, a letter opener? Dawn turned wildly around, casting her light everywhere she could to find a solution to her problem.

Her heart skipped a beat to notice the vent poised low upon the wall. The cover leaned beside it as though it had been in the process of repairs when the incident occurred.

Providence, working on her side! But would she fit?

Thankfully, she would. Not comfortably by any means. But, all the same, Dawn snapped the lighter shut and found she could just squeeze into the ventilation duct.

Not a moment too soon, either.

The door to the office opened behind her.

8.

ANDREA ASSESSED THE empty office with her arms folded over her chest. She was certain she had heard the sound of glass breaking, and she definitely found the broken glass in question.

But, by the time she managed to reach into the dark room and unlock the knob, whomever had caused the window's destruction had vanished.

And that was *vanished.* Really vanished.

As in, disappeared.

Andrea worried her top row of teeth against her lower lip and glanced about the office, seeing nothing. Her foot nudged some object as she stood on the threshold of the room. After kneeling, she felt around and touched a candle.

Was this the candle Mary had been holding? Andrea's stomach twisted with terrible possibilities.

She didn't want to think about that.

She couldn't afford to think about that.

Andrea had known Mary since elementary school. Their mothers were friends. To say they were like sisters was probably an exaggeration, and they had been far closer before Andrea got busy with middle school sports. All the same, they were very close... and the thought of Mary's screams from earlier cut through the athlete like a knife, even in the hazy fog of memory.

Yet, what had Andrea done?

Nothing.

Certainly nothing more than Chris, that coward. She shouldn't have expected him to be dependable in any way. While she searched the desk for a box of matches, groping around in the dark and hoping she might avoid encountering a spider, the volleyball player thought of her boyfriend's back receding into the darkness. He'd slowed for her, but that nun had come out of nowhere and they'd had to split up, losing track of each other. The nun had gone after Chris, and Andrea had escaped.

She just hoped he, like Scott and Mary, were still alive somewhere...and that Barbara and Dawn had already made it out and taken the car to go get help.

Not that Andrea exactly savored the thought of being stranded in a situation like this!

Andrea's fingertips brushed the rough edge of a small cardboard box. It rattled when she lifted it to her ear. She exhaled a breath she didn't know she'd been holding and slid the container open.

The match came to life with a sharp burst of sulfur that signaled relief from unrelenting darkness—and revealed Mrs. McDonnell standing in the doorway, her gaunt face still arranged that haunted expression.

Andrea nearly cried out, slapping her hand over her mouth to avoid the noise and only just keeping hold on the match. "Mrs. McDonnell," she said, gasping as she lowered her hand, "I'm so glad to see you! You were right—this place is dangerous."

Mrs. McDonnell looked grimly on while Andrea lit the blue candle. "I told you," the older woman said softly. "You wouldn't have believed me if I said anything more...but I still told you."

Shaking her head, Andrea whispered, "I'm sorry we didn't listen. Have you found Janie yet?"

"I'm still looking."

"You need to be careful! That crazy nun is somewhere around here. You've seen her, right?"

"Yes," said Mrs. McDonnell, her tone as grim as her expression. Pulling her coat tight around herself, the older woman looked over her shoulder. The faint lines of her face grew far more developed as she stared off into the darkness. "I'm so afraid for Janie."

"I know you are, Mrs. McDonnell." Looking hopeful, the volleyball player stepped forward. "What if we worked together? We could—"

But the woman was already shaking her head.

"Too much noise," she said softly. "I'm already afraid just being here with you. Janie must be on one of the other floors, so I'll go and check...but you and your friends need to leave right now."

"I'm sure everybody wants to leave just as much as I do, but we have to find each other first."

With a long, somehow dubious expression—one implying she doubted such a thing were possible—Mrs. McDonnell turned away from where she stood on the other side of the door and ambled back into the darkness. Biting her lip, glancing down at the matches in her hand, Andrea whispered, "Mrs. McDonnell, wait!"

The woman paused just before she disappeared. Andrea hurried to the door and leaned through the open frame, the matchbox on the offer.

"For you. These might be useful—it's not safe walking around in the dark in a place like this."

"You're right," said Mrs. McDonnell, enfolding Andrea's hand in hers and holding it for a few seconds of true gratitude. "Thank you—thank you so much. God bless you."

Smiling, Andrea patted her hand in return and watched her strike a match. Mrs. McDonnell, by the glow of this small light, wandered off into the darkness of the hallway and disappeared at the far northern corner.

Alone in the small room, Andrea returned quickly to the island of false safety provided by the light of the candle. While she leaned over the desk to pick it up, her eye was caught by the label of a folder left in the middle of the desk. With anything less steady than candlelight, its typewritten words would have been illegible.

Having seen them, Andrea was shaken to her core. She had to read them twice just to be sure.

For a fraction of a second, Andrea was awash with the impulse to dart to the doorway and call Mrs. McDonnell back.

Then she realized how little sense the presence of a thing like this made.

Hadn't the school been closed for something like thirty years?

"So then, how—"

The volleyball player's eyes widened while she opened the folder and rifled through its contents.

"How is this possible?"

The question had just left her astonished lips when the sound of running reached her ears. Fear bolted through her.

Damn! Why had she given Mrs. McDonnell all those matches? She couldn't put the candle out, but she was going to have to.

Pinching the flame with her fingers, Andrea crouched in the darkness and waited. The footsteps grew nearer every second.

They stopped near the door.

Half-hidden behind the desk, Andrea strained to listen. Whoever was there stood just outside. Looking at the broken glass, maybe.

Andrea cursed herself for lacking the courage to run through the door and in the direction opposite the footsteps. It might have saved her a meeting with the demon that waited for her.

The nun appeared in the doorway, the white fabric of its coif catching whatever light there was to catch and rendering it visible enough to leave Andrea cold with panic...but not as cold as she was when one long arm slid into the room. Spindled fingers clad in black furled around the knob and twisted it.

Andrea had to move quickly. She had seen the duct and scrambled for it, not even knowing if she could squeeze in. It was close—very close. The volleyball player was tall and well-structured, her broad shoulders making her a tight fit.

But when the door opened behind her, she found a way to force herself. With a twist of her knee and a push of her sneaker off the office floor, Andrea crammed herself into the vent and grimaced—then screamed.

The nun's blade slashed her Achilles' heel and inspired a pain that was unlike any she had felt.

Andrea screamed to feel her flesh hacked open and muscle exposed to air, burning air. All the same, she forced herself to carry on. The claustrophobic coffin of the vent was a happier fate than whatever the nun would afford her.

Gasping for air, unsure if she was suffocating or just so afraid of tight spaces that she only thought she was, Andrea dragged herself through the duct of the air conditioning system. Her ankle dripped blood behind her, the fluid marking a perfect red trail as she made her escape. Teeth clenched, she fought through the pain the way she would have in volleyball and squirmed along the metal duct, moaning in frustration and fear as she found herself at an incline.

How long would these vents go on? It was so dark, too! She had no way of knowing whether she was passing up junctures that might have ended her torment much sooner.

Junctures that might have permitted her a happier fate.

After a certain point, though, it wouldn't have matter what direction she went. Andrea's blood rushed in her ears and her head buzzed with terrible fear. No breath seemed to fill her lungs.

What if she died this way? What if they found her body trapped in the duct—worse, what if they never found it? She'd heard awful stories of kids who climbed into chimneys or trunks or abandoned refrigerators and disappeared, never to be found for years and years.

Then, decades later, somebody would be remodeling and discover a little skeleton.

Andrea shuddered, tears filling her eyes. Her panic made her hyperventilate. The faster she breathed, the harder it was to breathe. The harder it was to breathe, the more she panicked.

She had to calm down!

Shutting her eyes, Andrea tried to pretend she was somewhere else. She remembered being a kid, a small kid, and going with her family to some kind of fair on Halloween. Andrea had no problem doing the crawl-in haystack maze on that occasion! That was the same as this, wasn't it? No difference at all really, except for the medium.

And the stakes.

And what waited for her at the end of the duct.

At one point, she did navigate blindly into what she realized was a fork in the duct. Her hands discovered two choices for her. Finding the passage to the right just slightly wider, Andrea took it. She grimaced as each push off with her foot produced a nasty bolt of pain. Andrea was going to have to take a look at it when she could.

That moment came sooner than expected. Andrea realized after only a few seconds of looking that a light touched her eyes. Stirred by hope, managing an incomplete but wholehearted gasp of excitement, Andrea dragged herself toward what looked to be an open area on the other side of the ducts. She scrambled forward, wiggled her shoulders through the opening, and was so thrilled to push free of the vent system that she didn't even realize there was nothing directly beneath her until it was too late. Halfway out, she had nothing to support her hands.

Andrea fell into the pit beneath the duct opening, crying out as she dropped what was easily nine feet.

The hard blow as she hit the floor was shocking to say the least. Her head rattling like a gong, Andrea groaned and rolled upon her back. Her wrists stung with alarming pain and she thought she might have dislocated a knee, but she hadn't damaged her skull or her spine. Not that she could tell, anyway.

No matter what condition she was in, relief flooded her just to be out of those ducts. She even smiled through the pain like her coach had once taught her to do.

Yes! Freedom.

The first step to freedom, anyway. With an empty, sinking feeling, Andrea let her smile fade.

The only exit out of the room was the one that let her in.

Yes—the same open vent. Nine feet above her.

Andrea groaned and sat up, her knee and wrist both aching as she pushed herself upright to look around.

The narrow room was totally bare. Nothing, not even another vent, adorned any of the walls. Not a stick of furniture existed anywhere in it.

Any blood remaining in her face promptly left.

Marveling at how numb she could feel, Andrea felt around the walls for some kind of door.

Quickly, she was overwhelmed with a panic worse than even the one she'd felt in the ducts. A panic, and a new certainty. She would starve, or suffocate. Or maybe, like in a cheesy movie, the walls would close together and crush her to death.

"Help!"

Andrea hurried up to the wall beneath the open

vent, her fists pounding against the concrete despite the sting it caused her sprained wrists.

"Help," she cried again, "somebody help! I'm stuck in the vent! Hello? Hello? Can anybody hear me?"

She waited. Listening. Hoping.

"Hello! Please! I'm trapped in the A/C ducts. I need somebody to help me!"

Again, she waited.

This time, the duct above her clanged with the sound of movement. Was somebody turning on a vent somehow?

No.

Someone was coming for her.

Andrea's heart lifted with hope.

"I'm right here," she called, "in this weird concrete room. Be careful! If you don't stop soon enough, you might...fall in..."

The athlete's face darkened as the black veil of the nun steadily extended into view.

New tears spilled from Andrea's eyes. The hollow features of the nun were all the more obscured by the unlit chamber. It looked like it barely had a face at all. Had any of its features been visible, Andrea surely would not have discerned the least trace of humanity.

"Please," she whispered in the dark.

The nun's mouth opened, an abysmal black void that filled Andrea with dread.

Red fluid that seemed nearly black in the darkness splattered from the nun and across Andrea's face. She only thought it was blood for a few seconds: then the burning started.

"Oh, God!"

Andrea screamed as the acid seared her face, her hands lifting to instinctively wipe at the fluid but stopping just before contact lest they, too, be subject to terrible chemical burn. As her forehead, cheeks and, worst of all, eyes blazed with agony, another burst of fluid dropped upon her face.

Her next scream was quickly stifled when the acid splashed into her mouth and corroded the lining of her esophagus.

Now her hands, covered in the stuff and dissolving with the contact, did try to claw at her face. They only hastened the liquefaction of her soft tissue. She realized her mistake when she was suddenly no longer breathing through her nostrils, but the sides of her nose.

The already dark room grew all the darker as her eyes oozed from her skull. With another scream, this one rattling and torn but no less urgent than its forebears, Andrea collapsed on the floor in a growing puddle of her own liquefied flesh.

She had been right.

No one would ever find her.

9.

SOMETHING WONDERFUL HAPPENED to Dawn
while she navigated the air ducts of St. Cecilia's.

After taking a left at a certain juncture, Dawn
began to think about turning around. Had she gone
the wrong way? Was she going to die up here? The
awful system was so stifling! She was glad she was
petite, but between the tight quarters and the
stagnant, dusty air, even Dawn was having a hard
time breathing.

But then, the miraculous event occurred.

The air began to move.

Gasping slightly to herself, Dawn asked aloud, "Is
the power back on?"

The scent of thick dust worsened, of course, but the movement of the air helped her breathe a little and soothed a body she hadn't realized to be overheating in her panic. Best of all, she was moving toward the source of the cool air. If she could find the blower for the A/C system, she might be able to find conjoined ducts into other parts of the school.

Feeling in her heart that she moved in the right direction, Dawn hurried forward at a slightly faster pace.

Sure enough: here was the fan whirling the dust from its blades, and there, left and right, were her two options.

Another fork in the vents soon gave her some confidence. Confidence, and hope. The slightest variation in path made her feel like surely this vent system had to have an end. Surely, there would be someplace she could go to get out of this claustrophobic labyrinth.

Here she took a left and ended up finding several vents, none of which were open for her to exit through. In the end she finagled something resembling a three-point turn in order to get back to where she made her incorrect decision. Once more at the juncture, she wiggled straight through along the duct for some time. Eventually, she thought her eyes deceived her.

A light at the end of the tunnel!

Almost laughing, then finding quickly that she had no sense of humor left, Dawn wiggled through the tight but ultimately accommodating duct. With a gasp of slightly fresher (or, at least, more abundant) air, Dawn popped her head out of the open vent and found herself, to her surprise, in a small room intended for one child. The purple and pink fleur-de-lis wallpaper would have been cheerful anywhere else, but in that space and that school the effect was disorienting.

Then there was the layout of the room itself, which seemed to have been intended as a storage space of some sort. The lamp still blazing in that cramped and tiny quarter illuminated no furniture but a bed and a dresser.

Anything useful? Dawn hurried to the dresser and checked the drawers.

Nothing—nothing at all.

Nothing except a scrap of newspaper barely sticking out from beneath the dresser.

It was so out of place that she couldn't resist the urge to give it a glance. Quickly she found it to be an old ad for stockings. Dawn was about to drop it where she found it when she noted a child's barely legible scrawl in the light graphite of a poorly sharpened pencil.

Sorry I didn't write in forever.
Mother Apollonia found my diary.
She locked me in punishment.
I don't think I'll ever get out.
I finally found a piece of newspaper to write on.
She doesn't treat the other kids this way.
I want to go home.

A throb of sorrow pulsed through Dawn's heart to imagine a little kid writing something like that. How could somebody working in the service of God inspire such sorrowful thoughts in a kid? Lips pressed thin, Dawn slid the newspaper into her pocket without really thinking about it. She was busy thinking of something else.

Mother Apollonia. That sure was some name! For some reason it filled Dawn with instant dread...but maybe that was because her relationship with nuns would be forever altered when she made it out of this place alive.

The door to the room was metal. Nearly sealed shut, too, owing to hinges corroded by time and no doubt more than one leak in the room—but, with a few hard shoves, Dawn managed to get it open. The cramped room was at the very end of a half of them, the final door before the one that led to a dangerous-looking set of stairs.

Thunder cracked outside.

Dawn recoiled from the staircase—different from the one that let them into the building, it seemed—and thought it best to check through some of the rooms on the floor.

She had been right about the dormitory format. There were four such rooms on that floor, all of them blackened with blood when the light shuddered on for the first time in years. Many of the lights did not work, their sockets corroded beyond repair or the filaments of their bulbs having been permitted to burn out without replacement. The ones that did seemed dim and dingy, slow to activate and sorry to show her what they did.

Her stomach twisted in knots to look across the disarrayed beds whose unmade mattresses were black with the blood of children. What kind of monster could have done this? How was a thing like this even possible? She recoiled from the thought and the room at once, backing down the hall and looking elsewhere.

A shower room stood on this floor, just like on the

lower one. A metal operating table had been permanently installed in the farthest section of the red-tiled
chamber.

Dawn didn't want to know anything about that.

The more she looked around, the more she
began to think that the first floor—with its offices,
its classrooms, its hallmarks of a normal boarding
school—was designed to lull parents and students
into a false sense of security. No room sealed that
opinion quite like the weird medical ward she
stumbled upon.

From the second she flipped on the light, the
adrenaline was coursing through her in a more
traditional sort of fear. The nurse's station downstairs
had been simple and innocent. An infirmary as one
would find at any school.

The medical ward, however, was decidedly
Victorian in its appearance and perceived methods.
From the dental chair reclining in the center of the
room to the horrific array of metal picks, pliers,
scissors and needles, the medical ward was either a
location where the former instructors of the isolated
school dealt with severe medical issues on-site, or
where they practiced their war crimes.

Dawn just hoped they had a doctor on-staff...
otherwise, the answer was likely to be a combination
of both.

As far as useful items, the medical ward had less
than one might have thought. She was tempted to
take something sharp but couldn't help think an
impromptu weapon would instill exactly enough false
confidence to get her killed.

Besides...most of the implements on the shelves
or arranged around the counter of the nearby sink

were just as likely to break as they were to do any damage. The closet might have contained more that was of interest, but its knob refused to budge under her hand. Shaking her head, Dawn turned to exit the room while reaching for the light switch.

Something metal rattled to the floor.

Whipping rapidly around, Dawn scanned the room and tried to find what had fallen out of place. Had she brushed something with her hip, perhaps? The blood flowed out of her face to find there was nothing amiss.

Nothing she could see.

With a frightened glance at the shut door of the supply closet, Dawn edged quietly to the table covered in metal tools.

In the absence of anything reliable, what could she use to defend herself? A scalpel? Well...it was better than nothing, but it required such close proximity that it made her nervous.

And more nerve-wracking still was the thought that maybe it *wasn't* the nun in that closet. Maybe it was another assailant. Maybe it was even Mrs. McDonnell's missing daughter. If that last one were the case, Dawn had to make sure she wasn't going to accidentally stab an innocent girl.

To give herself a fighting chance and space to make a snap decision, Dawn told herself it was better not to open the closet on her own. She shut off the light, loudly walked through the doorway of the medical ward, then crept back into the darkness of the chamber and crouched in the corner by the counter.

Outside the room, the power failed again.

Five seconds later, the closet door creaked open.

10.

CHRIS WAS SOMETIMES accused of being a selfish person, but that was because most people didn't understand he lived his life by one simple rule. It was a rule that would have improved the lives of all the people judging him if they made it their own policy in all things.

The motto that Chris held near and dear to his heart was, "Work smarter, not harder."

An uncle had once delivered that sage wisdom. Chris had never been the same since. To call him lazy or cowardly or passive was just a misunderstanding of his actions.

Take, for instance, when he was driven from the dining hall by the nun and separated from his girlfriend as a result of their flight.

The way Chris saw it, Andrea could take care of herself. She was a strong woman, tall and densely stacked with muscle from constant volleyball matches.

There was no way she was going to succumb to any crazed nun wielding a chef's knife.

Not by being chased down, anyway.

Therefore, realistically, Chris was only going to slow her down if he tried to stick with her. So...when she went right, he went left.

To the car.

Theoretically.

We all knew what had happened to Kevin's Jeep by now. And poor Kevin. Poor Kevin! Poor Kevin, and poor Kevin's keys. Stuck sitting in the pocket of his dead body. Who could stand the thought of them brooding sadly in there?

Except...well. By the time Chris managed to get back to Kev's body, the keys had already been liberated.

Damn.

Uh—that was, good for them. Not that it was good Kevin was dead, understand! RIP, Kevin. Horrible stuff, absolutely horrible.

But Chris was focused on one thing, and one thing only: his own self-preservation. This was a basic matter of human existence. You couldn't do anything for anybody else if you weren't alive, after all! Couldn't go into town and tell everybody what happened. Couldn't call for the cops from the nearest phone booth, or co-author a best-selling account of your harrowing survival in the midst of untold danger.

Couldn't see how ahead of yourself you were getting...a tall order for somebody like Chris.

With Kevin's keys a non-starter, the next option that flashed through Chris's head was Barbie. He had heard a lot of shrieking and hollering from the school's entrance while he was hiding in the same stairwell where they came in. Chris could only assume that all the ruckus had a little something to do with, you know...Sister Bundy, or whatever this chick's name was.

So, he waited for things to get quiet. He checked on Kev. Then, Chris got focused on two tasks.

Item one: Find Barb and convince her to ditch this scene, assuming she hadn't ditched it already.

She still had her keys as long as she had her purse. And she would have her purse as long as she agreed the smartest thing to do was to leave immediately, risk the stormy mountain back to her car, and book it to town faster than even that fast-moving nun could follow.

A shudder rolled through him just to think of their assailant. To think of dying like Kevin, with his last moments on earth spent enduring the vicious stabs of a knife—ah, man!

No, way.

Chris just couldn't prioritize anybody other than himself. But, he liked to think that item two made up for it.

Item two: Find the generator or other power source, and do whatever it took to turn it on.

If the power was on, they stood a chance of finding some device that might permit them to communicate with the outside world. Furthermore, if the school had power in even a few circuits, they wouldn't have to worry about nonsense like juggling candles...though he wasn't sure how old the electrical system in the school was, nor how long it would be able to maintain that power.

And all this was theoretical, anyway.

Because, well...if there was no way to turn on the generator, and he couldn't find Barbie within twenty minutes or so, Chris was going to hit the road and take it slowly down the mountain until he found a sane person or made it to town with pneumonia.

Therefore, with a candle from the dining hall in his hand and Kevin's eyes respectfully closed, Chris hurried back down to the concrete stairs as quickly and as quietly as he could. On his way, he checked every door that looked likely. After three dead silent attempts during which the other wing of the school was filled with screaming that sounded uncomfortably like Andrea, Chris came upon a janitor's closet.

Allowing himself to emit a low whistle of relief, Chris sorted through the cobwebbed supplies arranged around him. A couple of screwdrivers, a pair of wire cutters, a handful of hex keys and some fuses. His eyes skipped across a bottle of turpentine and a few containers of various other cleaning supplies while his mind sought for anything that could be of specific use.

Nothing in the closet seemed particularly unsafe aside from the chemicals...though, he had to admit, it was strange.

Chris was a little bit of an artist—at least, he knew Barbie from a painting class—and turpentine, well... it did go bad after awhile. It got gummy, and took an off color.

This stuff, however, seemed fresh.

Something about this detail disturbed him. He recoiled from the closet with a shake of his head and shut it behind him before continuing on to the enclosed staircase.

Now...last order of business. Find a generator and a way to turn it on, then replace a few fuses and forget the candles.

The basement was a weird hallway, some kind of former cellar, maybe, enclosed with pale bricks. Here there were a few things—a room with an old, old, old washing machine that was so ancient it seemed to have been from the very invention of the device back in 1920. There was another room, a storage area for items that Chris assumed to have been confiscated in anticipation of parents reclaiming said items on behalf of their students when terms were up. There was an ancient furnace covered in dust and a lot of rat crap all over the floor.

And, most importantly, there was a big, beautiful, gas-powered generator not far from the fuse box. It was already hooked to the breaker with dusty wires that had mercifully evaded the nibbling of the rats. All that was really necessary was hoping there was an un-evaporated can of gasoline lying around.

Luckily for Chris, there was one more room there in the basement of St. Cecilia's. It was at the far end of the hallway...and it was locked.

But that was okay, because Chris liked a challenge.

While the vents above him made a weird rattling sound that made him wonder how deep the rat infestation had gotten into the school over the years of its abandonment, Chris hurried back up the stairs. Poised upon the landing of the ground floor, he paused to listen.

No sounds, other than the clanging and banging of the ducts over his head.

Shielding his candle from prying eyes, he made his way to the nearest office and rooted through the desk. A yellowing stack of typewriter paper yielded the paper clips he needed. Soon he was back at the door, feeling like an absolute genius for ever having learned the theories of lock-picking on a lark. To think anybody made fun of him for spending his time in libraries before dating Andrea!

With a hex key and only two paper clips, the first having snapped off while he explored the tumbler's pins, Chris managed to coax the locked basement door open. It swung wide for him and his eyes practically sparkled in the light of the candle he finally, regretfully, had to snuff for his own safety.

With a gas can in his hand—also as surprisingly fresh and un-dusty as the turpentine had been—Chris returned to the generator, filled it up, and got it started.

The moment he began monkeying with the breaker box and the basement lights came on was quite possibly the proudest of his life.

"There she goes," he said with pleasure, shutting the little door after a few other switches had been flipped. "See if you can sneak up on anybody now, you crazy bitch."

It was his one contribution, he figured—the one thing he could do for everybody, assuming they figured out the power was even on and had the good fortune of finding lights that worked. With the air conditioner running, (and making more clanging and banging than ever), Chris was sure his friends would figure it out.

Leaving his candle behind, Chris made his merry way back up the stairs. He now told himself he had five minutes to find Barbie or leave and face the rain.

He wasn't expecting to reach the landing of the first floor just as the nun opened the door to the still-dark stairwell.

Chris's skull went numb with fear as the nun rushed him with the knife in-hand. His scream was a competitor for hers, to say the least. The nun was so quick that the thought of pushing it down the stairs hardly even crossed his mind. As had been the case earlier, Chris became focused on one matter and one matter only: survival.

He was not as fast as Andrea, it was true. But Chris was still in reasonable shape, and he could still make a run for it with the best of them. Dashing up the stairs slowed him just a little, but he still managed to get a flight ahead of the madwoman.

One floor, two floors; stairs that implied a third floor. If Chris kept running a little more he might be able to make it to the next floor and find a room to hide in before the nun saw where he went. If he got off the proverbial ride on the second floor, well, she would almost certainly still be on his tail.

Pumping his muscles into high gear, Chis took the stairs two at a time in his sprint to the third floor. He hit the landing, careened around the corner—

And slammed face-first into a gate that had been pulled across the remaining set of stairs.

"What? No."

With a horrified gasp, Chris gripped the gate and gave it a rapid shake.

"No, no!"

He looked wildly for any sign of a latch.

Instead, he found a combination lock.

"No! No, no, no! Oh, God, no. Somebody help me—"

Andrea had produced a scream like that.

Mary before her.

Kevin hadn't had a chance to scream before his death.

And had Chris helped a single one of them?

Of course not.

So why should anybody have come to help him?

Boyish tears welled in his eyes as the nun's deliberate footsteps echoed up the stairs. He threw himself against the gate. A little hint of hope intoxicated him as the barrier rocked back against his weight, but the edges were securely bolted into the walls and impossible to break down without a lot of work. Work he didn't have time for.

Teeth clenched, Chris snatched the screwdriver from his back pocket and held it as though he were prepared to stab his pursuer. He was not sure that he could manage such a thing even to survive.

"Stay back, you hear me? I'm warning you, if you come any closer I'll—I'll kill you!"

The footsteps stopped at the third stair from the top.

Heart racing, eyes overflowing with tears, his nose rapidly sniffling snot away from his terror and grief-contorted face, Chris said, "I'll do it! Get out of here, go on! Just let us go, won't you? Why are you doing this?"

The nun's eyes locked with his as it careened around the corner, lurching into motion with the knife raised high. Chris screamed, his screwdriver dropping to the floor as he raised his hands palm-out in self-defense.

His eyes widened while his mouth produced scream that rattled the dark stairwell. Chris's own blood splattered hot across his face and, with him pressed back against the gate, the nun pinned him there to bury the knife in his gut again and again.

Chris's last word, as he stared into the empty face of the nun, was, "Why?"

The twelfth time pulling the knife out of him, Chris's killer tugged up.

While his intestines spilled upon the floor, Chris followed.

11.

WITHOUT AMBIENT LIGHT from the school, Dawn struggled to see who stepped out of the closet. She might not have figured it out if Scott didn't nail his shin on the edge of the dental chair while trying to make good his escape from the room. The unmistakable whisper of profanity lifted a leaden veil from Dawn's mind.

"Scott!" She gasped, leaping up from her place and provoking a shriek from her friend. Lifting the lighter and flicking it on, she enthused, "It's me!"

"Oh, Dawn!"

His hand upon his heart, Scott hurried over to embrace her. Dawn had to wonder if they'd ever even really shook hands...but who cared? The brief, reassuring contact with a friendly human being flooded her brain in a soothing cocktail of dopamine and oxytocin, doing a little to balance out all the adrenaline and cortisol from her high-stakes ordeal.

When the two separated, Scott's brow furrowed right way. Even in the dim glow of the lighter, his eyes brimmed with glistening tears.

"Mary," he said. "Mary's dead—God, what did I do?"

Dawn's heart clenched with pain at the thought. While Scott covered his face with his hand and tried to get it together, Dawn said, "You didn't do anything, Scott. You were just messing around."

"Yeah, but maybe I could have helped her. Maybe I could have done something, anything for her. It was horrible." Lowering his hand from his eyes to regard her wetly, he blubbered out the words, "Horrible, there—the stairs, the front stairs by the dining hall..."

Trapped, he said. A trap that he almost fell into, himself.

Scott's experience, as he related to Dawn, had been a highly traumatic one. After hearing Mary's final scream stop so suddenly, he had known for sure that something was wrong. Already, he'd had his share of doubts, but his pride had kept him from doing anything.

Now it was too late. Scott skidded around the edge of the staircase, made his way up the first flight, and mercifully caught a flash of wire in the brief illumination of lightning outside. He stopped short before tumbling into the razor pit where Mary's bleeding body lay tangled.

His first scream had been one of horror and anguish.

His second scream had been because the nun had appeared behind him to push him into the pit with Mary's body.

As immediately poised to fight as he had been upon the sight of Mary's dead body, Scott managed to act quickly enough to catch himself on the edge of the wall. In a fast spate of panicked motions, he had managed to dodge his assailant. Here, his eyes squeezed shut as he related the story to Dawn.

He had still fallen forward into the pit...but, thank God, atop Mary's body.

"I'm all scratched up," he said, showing Dawn a few bandaged cuts that he had patched up with the old, barely workable supplies in the second floor's operating theater. "But—but, thanks to Mary, I was able to get upright and just barely jump to the next flight of stairs. There wasn't anything else like that, like that barbed wire pit. I—God, Dawn, I had to step on her *head* to make it out. I felt her sink into the razors."

Here was to hoping that Mary really was already dead at the time.

Even in the dark, Scott had the distinct look of a man about to be ill. He braced himself against the cool surface of the nearby counter while telling Dawn weakly, "This is all my fault. I still feel like I'm dreaming...I wish I were, anyway. I just ran as far as I could from that whole scene and ended up on this floor. Well—really just in this room. Once I got myself patched up, I couldn't make myself leave."

Dawn knew the feeling. If she hadn't been desperate to find some kind of phone, or any other way to contact the outside world, she never would have gotten out from underneath the cot in the bogus nurse's station downstairs. It sounded like that nun was even more insane than Dawn had thought. Pits full of razor wire in the place of staircase landings!

What kind of maniac thought of something like that?

"I'm sorry about Mary," said Dawn gently, "but that means, if we can just figure out where Chris and Andrea are, we can go meet Barbara outside."

Hope stirred in his voice. "Barbie got out?"

"Yeah...I just hope she was able to find somewhere safe to wait. Between the storm and this crazy person running around, I'm still just as worried about her as I am about the rest of us."

"Well, did you see which way Chris and Andrea went?"

Dawn shook her head. "I don't know. We ended up on opposite sides of the school...I hope they're still alive." With a glance at the hallway, she continued, "Maybe one of them managed to get the power going? We should head down to the basement and take a look. One of them could still be there."

With an uneasy look, Scott said, "I don't know about those stairs. How are we supposed to get across the gap? Mary's body, and all..."

"There's that other set of stairs—the concrete ones we came in through, remember? I think those continued down to the basement. We could at least take a look."

After a few seconds of hesitation, Scott nodded.

"Okay," he said. "I feel better moving around here with the two of us together."

Dawn couldn't help her laugh. "You and me, both."

The laughter was about as short-lived as laughter could be, however. Any good feelings that arose as a result of Scott and Dawn finding one another, in fact, seemed to dissipate as they emerged through the door to the concrete stairway.

In the darkness of that eerily echoing space, the

flickering lighter illuminated two things: the black bars of a gate pulled across the top of the stairs, and the deep red pool of blood that had rolled out in all directions around the fulcrum of Chris's corpse.

Scott cried out and stumbled back from the sight, his stomach at last giving up. While he dashed out of the stairwell to puke in a corner, Dawn cried Chris's name out loud and received no response.

Gritting her teeth, she held the lighter before her and stepped gingerly through the pool of blood. She tried not to think about it too deeply and instead focused on maintaining her balance while squatting down to illuminate the body.

Chris was not a pretty sight. His entire front was stained red with the same blood that flowed around him. A screwdriver lay near his hand, soaked.

Well...it hadn't done him much good, but it was the closest thing to a weapon Dawn had yet seen.

Face arranged in a grimace, Dawn reached through the bars and stretched out her arm. With the very tips of her fingers, she coaxed the screwdriver toward the gate and to her position crouched on the other side. It took some contorting and a fair bit of discomfort, but gradually she was able to knock the screwdriver around enough to grasp the blade with her fingertips and drag it over.

"Thanks, Chris," she said sadly, too drained and too urgently focused on escaping the school to spend much time wallowing in grief. Touching the curly hair of the corpse through the bars was all she could manage; and that, only for a few seconds.

Then, with the bloody screwdriver in her hand and bright red footprints left in her wake, Dawn returned to the hallway. While wiping her feet off on the carpet and the screwdriver off on her shirt, she said, "Looks like we're going to have to try the other set of stairs after all."

Scott looked about to protest, but Dawn turned to lead the way there and calmly insisted en route, "We don't have to go all the way down. In fact, we should do a quick search of the second floor to see if we can find Andrea. Why don't we just go one floor down, then sweep back to this side of the school?"

"All right," he said weakly, clearly still less than thrilled by the notion of being in the same stairwell as Mary's body. "But—"

Dawn paused, peering through the dark at a face that was lined with concern like she'd never seen Scott wear.

"If we can't find her," he asked, "when do we call it quits?"

Inhaling, Dawn lowered her head. She studied the flame of the lighter.

"I don't know," she answered. "I don't know if I can make myself leave this place without at least knowing what's happened to her...I wouldn't want anybody to do that to me, after all."

"Yeah, but—if she's already dead, there isn't any more that can be done."

"But if she's still alive, we're abandoning her."

Scott fell silent at that, his jaw tensing—no doubt, with memories of Mary's final scream. After turning this over in his head, he slowly nodded.

"Okay," he said. "Okay, you're right. We can't abandon her if there's a chance she's alive."

Glad they were in agreement, Dawn led Scott down the hall. Together they descended what was intended to be the school's primary set of stairs.

Navigating together was something of a pain. The lighter's glow just wasn't that extensive. Scott had to stay pretty close to Dawn, and as a result the two bumped into one another frequently. Every little noise as a result of these impacts made Dawn's internal organs twist up in anxiety. Had their hunter heard?

Even better question: Did their hunter still have anyone else to hunt?

Because, well...Barbara was outside. Mary, Kevin, and Chris were all confirmed to be dead.

Janie and Mrs. McDonnell? Hard to say the status of the former; Dawn hadn't seen the latter for some time.

That meant, with Andrea's whereabouts unknown, Dawn and Scott were now prime targets.

In normal circumstances, this was where people began praying.

12.

THE SECOND FLOOR, Dawn and Scott found, was by and large devoted to two types of rooms.

One wing consisted of private rooms for the nuns who ran the school, and the other seemed to be largely devoted to classrooms far greater in number than the handful of showrooms on the first floor.

They checked the nuns' quarters first. Dawn had always pictured nun cells as being quite cramped, and these were not exactly the Taj Mahal. However, each room they entered seemed comfortably sized. Certainly fit with a more comfortable-looking bed than the ones given to the students.

Most of the rooms were undecorated save for crucifixes and books like old copies of St. Augustine's *Confessions,* or St. Teresa of Avila's divinely inspired writings. One of them, however—the largest, as well as the only one fit with a private bathroom—was clearly intended for the headmistress of the school, or Mother Superior, or whatever her title was. Like a queen in her own domain. She even had a view that revealed the continual raging of the storm, though by that point the only storm Dawn cared about was the one raging throughout the school.

Together they swept the room and found nothing of particular interest until, when discussing their plans to clear the classrooms, Dawn suggested, "Maybe this lady has an old map somewhere or something."

Cursing herself for not taking more time at the desk of that central office downstairs, the music student rifled through the Mother Superior's old paperwork and coughed as dust puffed up from the surface. While Dawn leaned away to calm her throat without making too much noise, Scott said, "No map...just some unsent orders for food and medicine. And..."

Scott fell quiet, lifting the letter toward his face to try to read it better in the lighter's dim glow. His face scrunched up, brow furrowed and eyes narrowed, before everything relaxed into a commingling of delight and astonishment.

He even produced a laugh.

Hopeful at once, Dawn asked, "What is it?"

"Look at this," he said, tossing it down on the surface of the desk. As Dawn bent her head over it, Scott continued enthusing, "It's a work order—a request for somebody to come and fix the mechanism to open the safe room."

Eyes widening, Dawn asked, "There's a safe room?"

"Apparently, somewhere. Look!"

Dawn leaned down, her attention primarily caught by the paragraph in its center:

We were told there would be no other mechanism required than to turn the hands of the grandfather clock backward to 4:00, but when we looked to see why the door wouldn't open, we discovered some of the clock's gears were rusted beyond repair. Is it true that the grandfather clock must function for the mechanism to work? If so, I must request that you return and assist us with the matter of fixing it, as we cannot do so ourselves. Please understand, this is a girls' school with an entirely female faculty. It is vital to our physical wellbeing that the safe room be accessible in the case of an emergency.

"This is incredible," said Dawn with a near-sob, her hand pressing to her mouth and then to her heart. "Do you think that crazy nun knows about this?"

Scott shook his head. "I don't know—but if there's one place in this whole school that's bound to have a radio, a telephone, anything? It's the safe room."

Nodding in agreement, Dawn asked, "But where are we going to find gears? And where's the entrance to the safe room?"

"I don't know," said Scott in deep contemplation. "Gears, gears...there must be something mechanical that we've seen. Something we could poach for gears. If we're lucky, they might even fit. Any typewriters?"

She shook her head. "I've seen typewriter paper, but I don't know if I've seen any actual typewriters. If they were here, I'd guess they were in the offices downstairs...which means they're probably long gone."

"Probably..."

Rubbing his jaw in contemplation, Scott stared blankly into the note as if willing it to offer a solution. The glow of the lighter glinted off the glass frame enclosing a painting of St. Lawrence being cooked to death.

Their answer sprang out of the reflection as much as out of the painting.

"The kitchen," Dawn said, looking over at him. "One of the rooms off of the dining hall was the kitchen. I looked in it and saw a big, industrial-sized scale!"

While Scott perked to hear such a thing, Dawn went enthusiastically on. "I have no idea if they'll fit, but it might have some gears. We could at least see what happens."

"That's a great idea. Ugh!" Scott shuddered. His spirits may have seemed significantly higher after such a suggestion, but his ability to cope with the situation was still no better than when he was puking in the hall. "We're going to have to go past Kevin, huh?"

"Yeah...let's just try not to look at him if we can't hear him breathing."

"And if we can?"

Dawn shook her head. "Then we'll have to find a way to get him to the safe room."

It wasn't a great plan, but it was a start. If nothing else, they could wait in the safe room for the storm to abate. Then, when walking down the mountain wasn't quite as suicidal as it would have been during the thunderstorm, they could make a run for it.

Dawn's mind churned in constant construction of plans while, out in the hall again, Scott gestured toward the other wing of the floor. "Should we check these rooms before we go down? They might have a grandfather clock that's more compatible, or something else we can use."

"Good idea. I'd sure like to find a candle or something."

Dawn would have appreciated that...but then again, if they had the capacity to split up, it would have been easy for them to be permanently separated.

Moreover, if Dawn had been opening doors on her own, she might have been the one to walk into the trap that got Scott in the end.

Dawn held the lighter, Scott opened doors. He wasn't thrilled about it, but after two empty classrooms they both became more confident that the nun wasn't lurking around every corner and waiting for her chance to strike. Not yet, anyway. After sticking their heads into a math classroom, a history classroom and then an old music room, Dawn said, "I don't know if there's going to be anything very useful over here, Scott."

"There's got to be something—a letter opener, anything—that I can use to defend myself if push comes to—"

The door to the science classroom had been slightly ajar. Scott opened it by casually shoving the palm of his hand against the edge of the wood. Dawn had barely enough time to cry out before the bucket of clear fluid splashed over Scott's head.

"Ah!"

His cry rang through the hallway, dwarfed in comparison to the clatter of the bucket upon the floor. While the metal pail rolled away, the young man grimaced and lifted his hands to his eyes. Crying out, he began to hurriedly wipe at them while a particularly acrid chemical scent filled the air.

Gasping, Dawn snapped her lighter shut.

"Turpentine," she said while Scott searched his shirt for a dry patch to rub against his eyes. "Are you okay? Did it get in your eyes?"

"I don't know, oh—ah, that burns—"

Looking around the room, Dawn rushed to the window and pushed it open with a noise of shock for how stubborn the old sash was. It rattled its way up the frame with a groan of protest, but the warped window did open enough to permit the storm's hammering down into the darkness of the classroom.

"Here," she said, hurrying over to Scott and guiding him, wincing, to the window. "Here, Scott, stick your face outside—"

"Ah—"

While the boy leaned out the window, his upper half suspended two stories above the ground and his face turned toward the patter of rain from the harsh black sky, Dawn kept a hold on his arm.

Even if he managed to get it off his face before getting a chemical burn, the turpentine had soaked his shirt. No way could she even think of using the lighter near him. They would have to move through the dark for now, it seemed.

Gritting her teeth, Dawn was about to suggest they focus on getting the lights on before activating the safe room. She didn't. Instead a greater, more terrifying thunder than any nature produced echoed through the second floor.

Sprinting footsteps came right for them.

13.

PANIC SURGED THROUGH Dawn at the sound of an approaching third party. She tugged on Scott's arm.

"We have to hide," she told him, inspiring him to move so quickly that he slammed his head on the windowpane. With a sympathetic wince to match his harsh grimace, Dawn dragged him behind the desk of the chemistry lab and crouched with him there on the floor.

A few doors down from theirs, the footsteps slowed.

One at a time, doors opened and shut after brisk investigation. The floorboards creaked as though to warn of the individual's approach even when they were not running. Dawn thought, with a sick twist of terror, of hiding beneath the cot in the nurse's office. Would she be lucky enough to avoid the nun the same way twice?

Luckily, she wouldn't have to.

"Janie?"

Scott and Dawn exchanged a look of relief through the curtain of darkness between them. Their bodies relaxed, all the intense fear of imminent conflict easing for the moment.

Mrs. McDonnell called again, her voice tinged with hope, "Janie? Is that you?"

"It's us, Mrs. McDonnell." Dawn stood, offering Scott a hand up from the floor. "Dawn and Scott."

"Oh!"

The bitter disappointment of her tone broke Dawn's heart. The poor woman was lucky she hadn't been caught by the nun yet...but Mrs. McDonnell was no doubt starting to think the same thing that Dawn feared.

Perhaps little Janie had not been so lucky.

Shoulders sagging in the doorway, Mrs. McDonnell's silhouette leaned back against the jamb. She rubbed her hand across her forehead. "I heard such a terrible noise! I thought for sure it was her. She's always getting into something..."

"No," explained Dawn, "it was us. The door to this room was trapped. Somebody put a bucket of turpentine on top of that door there."

With a noise of shock, Mrs. McDonnell took a step into the room before recoiling back to the hall. "Is that what all this is all over the floor? Oh, my—are you two all right?"

"Yeah, we're fine. I am, anyway—Scott got hit by it. How are your eyes, Scott?"

"They're not burning as much as they were about thirty seconds ago, if that means anything..."

Shuddering to hear such a thing, Mrs. McDonnell

held herself and wiped her shoe off on the floor. "This is all so awful. I just want to find Janie and get out of here."

"We're trying to do the same thing with our friend," said Dawn. "But—we just got some hope. There's a safe room somewhere in this school, Mrs. McDonnell."

Breath hitching, Mrs. McDonnell forgot all about the turpentine and stepped through it on her way into the room. "There is?"

Dawn nodded. "We're not sure where...but it seems like, if we fix the grandfather clock down in the main office, we should be able to access it. If we do manage to find it—if you hear the clock working or hear a door open somewhere—you and Janie should come hide in there with us until the storm winds down."

"That's so kind," said Mrs. McDonnell, her breath hitching more sharply as her composition began to dissolve. A soft sob wracked her words as she repeated, wringing her hands, "That's so kind! Oh, I want so badly to find my poor Janie."

"You will, Mrs. McDonnell."

But the worn-out lady shook her head. Slowly at first, then with increasing speed.

"No," Mrs. McDonnell said softly. "No, I'm afraid—I'm afraid Janie might be lost forever. Hearing all these screams, and seeing all this...the turpentine, the barbed wire pit...I don't think I'll ever be able to save her from this place."

"Don't think that way!"

Tired of suffering—tired of feeling that way, herself—Dawn hurried around the desks through the dark and caught Mrs. McDonnell's unready hand. The woman jumped in surprise but allowed herself to be touched, listening as Dawn went on.

"You have to believe that a way out is possible," the young woman told the older one. "You have to believe that you can survive—that there are alternatives for you to dying here just because some crazy person hurt you. I believe you can survive…I believe Janie can survive, too."

Stirred, Mrs. McDonnell asked, "Do you really believe that?"

Dawn nodded. "I do. Just the fact that you're still standing before me makes me believe that you'll make it through all of this alive. We all will."

Her lips parting in a weak smile, Mrs. McDonnell said, "You're a kind girl, Dawn…thank you. If—if you two go into the safe room without me, how will I find it?"

The teenagers explained what they had found in that letter to the handyman, describing the process of turning the grandfather clock backward to 4:00.

"I guess if we can't figure out where it is," summarized Dawn with a shrug, "then we'll just turn the clock back and try to listen for something mechanical somewhere."

Looking amazed to hear such a thing, Mrs. McDonnell nodded and said, "All right. If I can find Janie and the clock is running, I'll do that. Otherwise…"

"Otherwise, if you get to the clock and it's still not fixed, just hide nearby and wait for us to meet you there."

Satisfied by this, Mrs. McDonnell nodded again. After brief hesitance, she held both Dawn's hands in hers.

"God bless you, Dawn," she said warmly, her face almost glowing in the dark with her gratitude. "Thank you, thank you for helping me like this."

With that, Mrs. McDonnell left to continue the search for her daughter.

Dawn couldn't help but think to herself that it was truly amazing that aamazing a person could believe in God after experiencing St. Cecilia's Preparatory School.

Alone with Scott again, she asked, "Are you sure you're okay? Should we try to find you a new shirt?"

"Probably—but to be honest, I just want to get to that safe room. Plus, I don't know what they have to offer in the way of clothes…not exactly thrilled to change into a nun's habit."

Snorting humorlessly at that, Dawn shook her head and said, "All right. Well, since we're going to have to take the back stairs, let's hit the basement to get the lights on and then go check the kitchen."

Nodding, Scott said, "Good idea," and let Dawn lead the way around the turpentine puddle.

Thankfully, that crazy nun was nowhere to be seen as the two made their way down two flights of stairs. They soon found themselves in the same brick basement where, unbeknownst to them, Chris had been not long before. A red canister once filled with gasoline sat nearby. Seeing the generator was already fueled, Dawn urged her flammable friend to the side of the room and used her lighter to illuminate the breaker.

A few switches later and the basement lights flickered eerily on.

Dawn and Scott exchanged a sigh of relief while she shut the door. She frowned. "I wonder why it failed last time?"

Scott spread his hands.

"Ancient circuits overloading, not working? Or

maybe just, you know..." He lifted his eyebrows and glanced all around as if to indicate their assailant.

While Dawn pocketed the lighter, she realized with a start of fear that Scott had a point. Surely the nun would be attracted to the basement by the activation of the breakers. Chastened, she glanced at her friend and removed the screwdriver from her back pocket.

"Well...then we need to be ready."

Scott sighed and shook his head. "I'd like to be! Can we please find me something I can use to defend myself?"

"I think I saw an open utility closet at the end of the hall," she told him in response, hurrying to the doorway and peering out before waving him through. "There might be something in there that you can use in a pinch."

There was, thank goodness. A few seconds of looking about the closet revealed a wrench that might prove handy for getting the gears removed, and a hammer that might aid in more than one task... including one that involved the killer nun's skull. The two friends exchanged a look of gratitude and a sigh of relief while Scott took the dusty tool from where it lay beside a shovel and some old hedge clippers.

"That's perfect," said Dawn with approval. "We can even use it to get a few boards off of the courtyard door and lay a plank or two down across that razor pit."

Scott paled at mere mention of Mary's place of death.

"I don't know," he said weakly. "Can't we just use the back steps?"

"You really want to keep coming back here every time we have to go from the first floor to the second?

And then all the way back to the other side of the school to get to the third floor?"

"Maybe we could do something about that gate," he whispered, continuing to peck through the contents of the closet. "Come on...this is good, but I'd take a crowbar..."

"Scott, hurry it up." Tapping her friend on the shoulder, Dawn fidgeted toward the echoing chamber of the back staircase. "We have to go."

"All right," he said with a sigh, "all right, already."

Quietly as they could, the pair hurried to the stairs and began the long ascent. Scott led the way with his hammer at the ready, a bit of bravado in him now that he had something with which he could feasibly defend himself. Dawn was more than happy to let him take the lead for a few minutes, but she had to admit she was about as skeptical of his fighting abilities as she was of her own.

They reached the landing before the first floor and paused to glance up the next flight of stairs.

Dawn wasn't sure why, but something seemed wrong.

Scott didn't seem to agree and mounted the next set of steps.

The strike of a match echoed through the high chamber and made Dawn's heart race.

"Scott," she urged, "watch out!"

Too late. The nun swept into view and tossed a lit match upon Scott's turpentine-infused shirt.

14.

THE FRAYED SCENT of burning hair—and, seconds later, cooking flesh—spiked its way into Dawn's nostrils. Scott's scream rose through the stairwell as he was immolated head to toe in the golden blaze of the match. Hammer falling from his hand while Dawn recoiled, Scott thrashed and shrieked in mortal agony that was truly nightmarish to behold.

Just imagine what poor Scott went through while experiencing it! Dawn had never considered him to be a great guy by any stretch of the imagination, but he wasn't an entirely bad guy, either. She certainly didn't think he or anybody else who died that night deserved such awful fates.

But, as he dashed up the stairs, careening around the corner and after the nun who went flying away from the screaming human torch, Dawn couldn't help but think of a common phrase of her mother. This was one she said when witnessing a news story about a tragedy or hearing some unfortunate gossip about a relation.

There but for the grace of God go I.

It meant nothing to Dawn all the times she'd heard it before...but there, in the hallway, swaying in delirium to think how narrowly she had avoided the horrific fate of being burned alive, she could not help but reflect on that saying with more consciousness.

Had Scott not gone first into the science lab, she would have been the one burned to death.

Chilled by the thought, Dawn tarried just long enough to grab the hammer. Then she rushed up the stairs, not worried about making too much noise for the time being. Her friend screamed down the hall and after the nun, who had darted into the second floor and unfortunately headed in the same way Dawn had intended to go.

Just as the killer darted around the corner, Scott ducked into a nearby classroom. No doubt he intended to fling himself through a window...in which case, he would die in the rain and the mud, instead of the dust and the horror.

But Dawn was not going to die.

She was committed to it now. And still afraid, yes—but now, she was angry. Now Dawn hurried as quietly as she could down the hall, taking her chance to pause by the courtyard door.

Three boards blocked her way. Before she could think about working the nails out of even one of them with Scott's newly-acquired hammer, the nun's footsteps echoed down the hall with clear intent to either see where Scott went and finish the job, or discover where Dawn had gotten to.

Moving quickly and quietly, Dawn slipped around the corner and made her way up the eastern hall. Soon enough she found the rear entrance of the dark dining hall, where Kevin's body lay in a coagulated pool of still drying blood.

His face moved. Her heart skipped in horror for him. Was he still alive?

She took up one of the candles still burning on a nearby table and drew closer to her friend.

The rat that had been gnawing through his uvula, hearing her footsteps or feeling them rattle through its dinner, wiggled out of Kevin's mouth and scurried into the dark.

First, Dawn shrieked.

Then, Dawn realized what she had done.

Blowing out the candle and taking it with her, Dawn sprinted into the kitchen's swinging double doors. She had to hope that they shut behind her soon. In the meantime, she had to find a place to hide.

The kitchen was a special mess after all the years of neglect. Rusted and full of trash, it had a few likely hiding places...and then, she remembered her own prior thought about the scale and how disturbingly human-sized it was.

Breath seizing as the rear entrance to the dining room opened, Dawn grasped a nearby flour sack that had long-since spilled most of its contents. Even so, it was still surprisingly hefty. Gritting her teeth, she tugged the dense burlap cloth up into her arms.

Footsteps drew toward the kitchen doors.

The scale whined softly beneath the combined weight of a human being and half a wholesale bag of flour.

Dawn drew her foot into the protective covering of

the sack just as the kitchen door slammed open.

As they had when she hid under the cot, Dawn's eyes shut.

The nun stepped slowly into the room. Dawn swore she could feel its eyes trailing around, its single-minded obsession over hunting down her and her friends inexplicable as it was demonic.

After casting its first long stare around the room, the nun made its slow way around the shelves and the counters, the tables and the sinks.

What was wrong with this person? Clearly, whomever it was, they were the same person who had committed the first massacre...that, or they were closely inspired by it.

Or something else.

Hadn't Dawn just thought of the nun as demonic, after all? While a table screeched viciously across the floor and Dawn exhaled slowly through her mouth to keep herself calm, the girl couldn't help but think that there was something almost superhuman about the speed and endurance of the nun. If it was human, it had some kind of serious mental problem that kept it from recognizing its own fatigue.

Then again...didn't it go without saying that the person doing this had some kind of mental problem?

Upon making its way around the circumference of the room and determining Dawn was neither in the pantry nor under any of the counters, the nun left the room without delay and hunted for the girl elsewhere.

Dawn, trying not to cry, forced herself to remain where she was for another handful of long minutes.

A good thing she did. When she got up from the scale and shifted her weight up, the adjustment in her position made the poor old device gasp its final proverbial breath. With a terrible groan, a sharp little clang and the fatal twang of a spring, the cradle of her hiding place collapsed upon the base of the scale.

Something bounced out of the now disjointed pieces. Moving quickly to compensate for the amount of noise made, Dawn lit her candle and tried to find out what it was.

Wouldn't you know it!

A few bright, shiny gears.

Well...that might have been an exaggeration. They weren't exactly bright and shiny, but the important thing was that they weren't rusty.

The trick now was deciding how and when to open the safe room, and determining just where that safe room was. Dawn longed again for a map and wondered if the central office would have one that showed the safe room. Seemed like, either way, she was going to have to go to the uncomfortably exposed space of that office with its broken window.

That could be dangerous. Whatever needed doing to the grandfather clock needed doing quickly, and Dawn needed to get there quickly in addition. The collapse of the scale may well have just attracted the nun's attention back to the dining hall, if not to the kitchen itself.

But it seemed that there were other plans in store. Dawn stepped into the dining room in time to hear glass shattering from about the distance of the chapel. Andrea? Mrs. McDonnell, or maybe Janie?

Dawn wanted to investigate, but couldn't take the time. She couldn't risk crossing paths with the nun, either. For now she just had to be grateful for the distraction...and she could even repay the favor. If there was somebody in trouble in the chapel, the grandfather clock would just as likely prove a distraction in turn.

Heading in the direction opposite the noise, Dawn made her swift way down the hall. She ignored her urge to glance up the stairs toward Mary's body. Instead she hurried along the offices, slipped inside the one that had proved the focus of so much attention, and looked around the desk. After setting down the gears, Dawn slid open a couple of drawers. She flipped through an empty file that sat on top and seemed to have had its label sticker ripped off. She rifled through an address book from decades ago. She searched almost endlessly through the odds and ends littered about.

She did not find a school-sanctioned map...but she found something interesting nonetheless.

"A diary?"

The words rose from her in a whisper as she lifted the little pink book from a long-shut drawer. Carefully, Dawn turned the object over in her hands.

Mother Apollonia found my diary.

She locked me in punishment.

Was this the diary of the same child who had written on the back of that newspaper ad? Dawn couldn't help but suspect that it was; curious, not expecting to find anything of any particular value, she thumbed through the book.

The first entry she read, somewhere near the quarter point of the filled pages, seemed like something she would have expected from a Catholic boarding school.

Mother Apollonia told me I'm not praying enough.
This is the prayer I'm supposed to try:

The LORD is my light and my salvation. Whom shall I fear? The LORD is the strength of my life. Of whom shall I be afraid? Hide not Thy face far from me. Put not Thy servant away in anger. Thou hast been my help. Leave me not, neither forsake me, O God of my salvation, for He gives me the power to always see Thee.

It was normal to teach a kid to pray when they were afraid or sick or going to bed. That was the job of a nun. But then there were other, weirder entries— awful things. Shocking things. Certain words caught Dawn's eye. Soon, forgetting about the sound of the shattered glass, she found herself rapidly skimming through a diary that described corporal methods of behavior correction, public humiliation, and "punishment," which seemed to be isolation. The diary ended abruptly—Dawn supposed this was when Mother Apollonia confiscated it.

Lips pursed, she flipped back to the first page to gain some insight into the reasons its author was there. Instead, Dawn found two things that made her more interested than ever. The first was a page simply labeled, *I drew a map so I wouldn't get lost.*

Gasping, Dawn squinted at the rudimentary sketch. She soon recognized the shape of the first floor along with its many rooms. Perfectly symmetrical...except that, looking at the kitchen, she couldn't help but notice a lot of extra space available with respect to the dining hall. Now that she thought about it, the latter was about twenty feet wider than the other. That was worth thinking about.

Across from the map was another religious entry...

but, despite being so much earlier, this one was much more shocking.

Dear Diary,

Mommy dropped me off at my new school. I'm going to miss my old friends. I brought Bongo with me though. We have a teacher named Sister Euphemia. She has an assistant named Sister Odelia. They're teaching us all about the saints and what wonderful lives they lived.

Today we learned about Saint Lucy. Her eyes were put on a plate and she became a martyr. That's a weird word. Sister Euphemia said that her love for God saved her from the evil Romans that tried to hurt her.

Sister Rose said Mother Apollonia is going to take care of us.

Sheesh! That seemed like pretty graphic stuff to be teaching young kids. Sister Euphemia, though—Dawn knew that name! That was the aunt of Barbara's that died in the massacre.

And...she knew another name, too.

I brought Bongo with me though.

The name of the author uttered from Dawn's lips in a whisper.

"Janie?"

A feminine scream rang through the school like the tolling of a death knell.

Another.

Another.

Even across the distance of the school and through the lens of those three terrible screams, Barbara's voice was crystal clear.

Dawn dropped the diary and leapt from the desk, snatching the candle as she rushed off to the chapel. The hammer was clenched in her hand the whole way. Her arm trembled, but only with its readiness to use her weapon at any second.

There was no hesitation in her about what she was willing to do to defend her closest friend; no question of whether she was willing to take the life of the evil person responsible for so much death.

Impromptu weapon at the ready, Dawn rounded the corner, dashed through the dark, and soon burst into the chapel entirely without ceremony. The whole time, she was ready to meet the nun. Every shadow made her wince. Every rat risked dying by her hammer.

Yet, as the chapel doors flung open and she crossed the boundary of the allegedly sacred space, Dawn did not find the murderous assailant who plagued them that night.

She found only Barbara.

The stained glass windows in the chapel were broken now. Wind howled into the dark room and blew Dawn's hair about her face. She knelt before Barbara's body. Her friend died supine upon the three short steps leading to the altar.

Barbie's eyes had been gouged from her head, and the remaining flesh pits streamed gore that looked black in the darkness of the chapel.

For the first time in what seemed to be a century of all this horror, Dawn was overwhelmed by tears. Her arms encircling the limp form of her closest friend,

Dawn forced herself to look into the body's mutilated face.

This was what happened because she delayed. This was what happened because she had failed her friend. She sobbed, caressing Barb's hair and holding her limp hand.

"I'm so sorry, Barbara," whispered Dawn, looking at the terrible fate that had befallen her only because it would dishonor Barb's suffering to look away. "I'm sorry I didn't get out here sooner...I'm sorry. We should have tried going down the mountain. Barb! Oh!"

Heartbreak was real, Dawn learned then. She had always thought it to be a figure of speech, but the pain she felt in her chest was truly like nothing else. It felt like a canyon had been bored into her torso: a deep, twisting ache beaten in by the cascade of losses that the night had inflicted not just upon Dawn but upon her friends, her friends' families, and everyone else they knew.

And just feeling such things for other people made her realize that someday, somewhere, somebody would feel that for her.

The thought of her own death turning her fingertips numb, Dawn once more steeled herself. She may have been doomed to die one day...but she wouldn't let it be here.

Lowering her friend's dead body upon the stairs where she lay again, Dawn looked around for Barbara's keys.

Instead, Dawn noticed something beneath the dead body. Something that made her wonder if she had finally lost it.

Blood chilling, Dawn reached under Barbie.

She drew the item out.

The final pieces of a truly insane puzzle fell into place.

15.

ALL BARBIE WANTED was to have a good time with her friends. Maybe she was a little stubborn about it, sure. But did stubbornness mean she deserved to be responsible for this? Was this really the punishment she wrought upon herself and her friends—and all because she hadn't wanted to turn home and let them remember their last party together as a failure?

Of course...now they wouldn't remember anything at all, ever again.

Her business-savvy father would have been disappointed to know the sunk cost fallacy was his daughter's real killer.

Barbie trembled in the driving rain, her arms wrapped around herself and her purse locked tight in their embrace.

The storm was terrible! This weather was to blame for the night, not her. It had been cloudy when she left the house that night. By the time they'd picked up Dawn, a drizzle had begun over their little town. But, on the mountain roads, the already treacherous drive was further imperiled by the brutal thunderstorm that shrouded the mountain in a black veil.

If this rain had begun any sooner, or been mentioned in the forecast at any point, Barbara would have called the whole thing off. But when a freak weather pattern comes on so fast, well...who could blame her for thinking it was just going to be a quick burst of precipitation?

Look at Barbie.

Making excuses.

Did she really need to? Ultimately, Barbara was just being a teenager. She hadn't known. She had it in her head that the coolest place for a party would be an allegedly haunted boarding school. If you were trying to do something cool, one of the most un-cool things to do was cancel or back out at the last minute. It was a horrible thing to imagine being remembered for one last embarrassing failure of a would-be party, and Barbie just couldn't handle that.

Barbara had to admit it. She felt a crushing amount of pressure to be perfect. Why bother getting into it? People felt the drive to perfection for all kinds of reasons. Barbara had plenty of her own and was embarrassed by the impulse because, well...she was human. Humans were imperfect. And, why, she was fine with the imperfections of others.

But when it came to herself, she just couldn't accept anything less than the absolute best one hundred percent of the time.

There was no pleasure to be derived from taking such a hyper-critical stance toward oneself. It became a loop, in fact. A lifelong effort at outdoing every past attempt. When somebody lived like that, they were doomed to be unsatisfied in just about every regard... and found themselves doing ridiculous or even stupid things in the name of maybe, just maybe, reaching the day when they would finally uncover the thing that would satisfy them. They followed every vision, and anything less than a perfect manifestation of their personal will was a disaster in their sensitive minds.

So, Barbie had ignored the warning signs and pushed on with her friends to the top of the mountain.

And now Kevin was dead.

Crouched in the rain, Barbie cried for her dead boyfriend. Oh! Kevin was such a nice person. He had his flaws, of course—he could make fun of people a bit too much, for instance, and could be very critical of the faults of others—but he was also a very smart, very strong person. The type to take charge in any situation that needed a leader.

Which, of course, had been the cause of his death... at least, in part.

Kevin! The mere thought of his name made Barbie sob, her tears indiscernible from the rain. She wanted to stop weeping and instead think about something she could do; but, never having had a panic attack before, Barbie struggled to get her emotions under control at that precise moment.

Nothing like this had ever happened before. She'd never seen a dead body. She didn't like horror movies. All her grandparents were still living. The only pets who had died during her lifetime had been a pair of goldfish and a rabbit, the rabbit being a death from when she was too small to remember. Barbara was not used to accepting the darker realities of life and, similarly, was not used to any kind of danger.

She was not used to surviving.

Maybe that was what lured her to the boarding school in the first place. It was a place where girls younger than her had been forced to experience a modicum of independence, for better or worse. These girls managed to navigate the same circumstances Barbie dreaded.

The truth was that she was terrified of leaving her small town to go to college; terrified of leaving her friends behind. Mary and Andrea were important to her...and Dawn, especially.

Barbie loved Dawn. She wasn't sure Dawn realized how genuinely Barbara felt the friendship...nor how cool Dawn seemed to her. The truth was that Barbie admired the quiet musician.

After all—Dawn somehow managed to go through life without worrying what people thought of her. She managed to be talented, smart, and pretty darn funny. All without ever trying too hard, or getting down on herself, or obsessing over how she was perceived by her classmates. Dawn was very different from Barbara...and that was what Barbara liked about her from the start.

Now Barbie was more grateful for her friend than ever before. Dawn had been the reason Barbie got out of that awful school.

Now, like the rest of them, Dawn was trapped inside. Left to fight for her life against the insane person dressed, of all sacrilegious things, as a nun.

Barbara's stomach tightened to think of it. Who was this murderer capable of producing screams of mortal anguish so loud that Barbie, outside the school, managed to hear at least two of her friends' deaths over the rain? What did this evil person want? Was there any way to make them stop?

It seemed like Barbara was out in that storm for at least an hour. Maybe more. Her body shook in the cold downpour and each clap of thunder made her jump out of her bones. There was no place for her to seek shelter, either. Trees were out of the question with all the lightning. The overhang of the school's roof was too high to offer her any comfort.

And, anyway, she didn't want to be too near the school. Doing so would attract the attention of the nun. The longer Barbara stood in a doorway or under a side porch's covering, the more frightened she became. Soon enough she would withdraw into the darkness of the storm again, her teeth chattering fast enough to bite her tongue.

More than once she checked the remains of Kevin's car as if hoping to find it somewhat drivable. Resurrected. Even with the rain, the metal remained too hot to touch.

After checking Kevin's car, she would walk to the edge of the property and assess the wet highway around the curves of the mountain. Each time, she would consider making her way down its winding road.

Then, inevitably, Barbie would imagine twisting her ankle, or slipping and falling to her death, or being caught in a landslide, or being hit by a car that didn't see her. Beneath the pressure of these thoughts, she would retreat and weep again, utterly paralyzed.

Unlike most of her friends, Barbie was a Christian. Like most Christians, she hadn't prayed in years. Yet there, in the pouring rain, Barbie knelt in the mud and prayed to God.

Wasn't there something He could do? Was this some trial for all of them, one of them, none of them? Was this just some horrific random circumstance? Surely not. If not, perhaps this was somehow related to that awful night when her own aunt, Sister Euphemia, was slain by an evil killer still unknown to this day.

Or, perhaps...perhaps this killer was the spirit of Euphemia, an innocent nun returned from the grave and driven by hatred for the world she left.

It sounded ridiculous, but Barbie didn't know what to believe anymore. In a world where even Kevin could be senselessly murdered, all number of horrible things were possible. Everything now had the eerie, consequence-free quality of a bad dream.

Her friends had not come outside, after all. Barbie couldn't help but suspect that their absence indicated a fate as awful as Kevin's had befallen each and every one of them. She paced in the rain, colder than ever, her mind and body aching with each relentless droplet.

Gradually, as the minutes wore on and her frantic mind rushed in the midst of what may well have been increasingly dangerous hypothermia, she began to convince herself that the theory about Sister Euphemia's ghost was true. Some kind of family curse—a punishment for Barbie and her failure to make the right choice. To turn around.

The weight of the responsibility became suffocating. The spirits of her surely dead friends seemed to gather themselves around her and mock her for wasting their lives. For being the reason they made it eighteen years and then died abruptly, violently, in a place where no one could have possibly helped them.

Steeped in panic, paranoid delusions, and the brutal effects of cold mountain rain upon the human body, Barbie was at last chilled by the sound of Scott's awful scream. It ended in sudden wet silence.

She couldn't stand it a second longer. If she didn't get into that place and help her friends, she was going to go insane.

Finding a suitable rock, Barbara circled around the school and tried to get her bearings. She wasn't sure exactly how things were oriented after all her hovering about in the rain. The only windows that had an immediately obvious room attached were the stained glass ones that marked the chapel.

Gritting her teeth, Barbie hurled the rock.

The multicolored glass crumbled within its tall frame, tinkling down upon the floor of the chapel like a shower of stars. Grimacing as a few shards scraped her hand, Barbara nonetheless braced against the edge of the open frame and climbed inside. She stumbled into the darkness of the room and lingered for a few seconds, permitting her eyes to adjust.

Here it was. A room that, in another time or place, would have been beautiful to her. Safe to her. Somehow the chapel felt to Barbie like the most unsafe room in the world now, but it did help to get her oriented in the school. She knew roughly where it was located based on Dawn's description. If she could just find Dawn herself, and anybody else, maybe they could help each other out of this terrible place and down the mountain with the safety of numbers.

When she could at last perceive some of the objects in the room after about a minute of waiting, Barbara made her cautious way around the pews. She quickly found the cabinet of candles that Dawn had previously plundered. Plenty remained. Barbara took up a votive and groped around the surface of the cabinet before finding a box of fireplace matches.

She lit her candle and sighed in relief at the light. A small relief compared to the depth of the oppressive darkness around...but a relief, nonetheless.

Before she left, Barbara looked at the statue of the crucified Christ as though to appeal for His help.

Something seemed wrong.

Barbie wasn't sure what it was. The position of the figure upon the cross seemed somehow distorted. Weathered wood, maybe?

No...the chapel had been perfectly dry before she broke the window. That was easy enough to tell.

Frowning, Barbara edged toward the altar and lifted her candle toward the image of the crucifixion.

The flickering flame of the votive in her hand illuminated a woman's withered corpse, decades old and long-since suspended upon a cross in place of Christ.

Barbie's scream rose high in an instant, leaping from her throat and unstifled by the hand that formed a kind of claw before her mouth.

The door creaked open behind her and she unleashed her second scream. Barbara turned in time to see the nun rush at her.

Acting on pure instinct, Barbie threw the votive candle. It shattered on the floor behind the nun, who was upon her in a second. A third scream rose from her before the nun gripped her by the throat and squeezed her windpipe so tightly that Barbie felt it collapse. The sting was so sharp and immediate that it felt as if she had swallowed some of the glass from the broken window.

She certainly fell back into some of it as the nun's pressure forced her upon the floor. Moving her mouth as though to cry out, Barbie thrashed and pushed at her killer's surprisingly light body. She shoved the nun's face and slapped its cheek, and soon enough began raking her fingers in. The killer made no noise, but did lift its hands to fend off this weak defensive assault.

As if inspired by Barbara's attempt to defend herself, the nun sank black-gloved thumbs into the inner corners of Barbara's eyes with slow, deliberate pressure.

Barbie screamed in mortal agony. She pushed at the nun and gripped the black cloth of its habit. Her eyeballs burned and her brain ached and she kicked and fought and tore at her assailant with all her might.

And it wasn't good enough.

Barbie gripped a fistful of something soft. Whatever it was, she felt it pull away from her murderer while her eyeballs burst out of the exterior corners of their sockets. The orbs—or what remained of them, at any rate—drooled down her cheeks while, open mouthed, she stammered in silent agony.

Her killer's footsteps trailed away.

Unable to obtain air through her destroyed windpipe, Barbie collapsed beneath the overwhelming gravity of death.

As her head fell back, someone rushed in with a cry.

Thank God, Dawn was still safe.

16.

DAWN STOOD OVER Barbie's dead body and stared at the doll in her hand.

Bongo the Clown leered back at her expectantly. Its bucktoothed features mocked her.

Grinning.

Waiting for her to understand the punchline of the hideous joke.

And—yes. Now, she understood.

Nothing had been making sense. Janie, lost somewhere in a school in the middle of nowhere, in a place where a little kid had no reason to be. Mrs. McDonnell, wandering listlessly through the halls of St. Cecilia's Preparatory School, somehow managing to avoid the nun. Bongo the Clown, Janie's toy, appearing everywhere. In the diary. At the site of a murder.

In Mrs. McDonnell's possession.

They were all the same person.

Mrs. McDonnell, Janie, and the nun.

In fact...

...Had Mrs. McDonnell ever said that Janie was her daughter?

Trembling, Dawn nearly threw the doll as far away as she could. That was certainly her impulse, if nothing else. But, at the same time, she was somehow grateful to the creepy, smarmy little toy.

Because, much as it showed her the way to the candles the last time they met, now it illuminated a truth so powerful that all Dawn's fear dissipated.

There was no room for fear when a person overflowed with so much anger.

Did Jane McDonnell understand what she was doing? Was this a case concerning an absolute psychopath, or a complete psychotic? Dawn didn't understand much about formal psychology, but she did understand that there was crazy...and then there was evil.

So which one was Jane McDonnell, who dressed up like a nun to kill intruders on the old property where she once laid waste to a whole school of people?

Dawn thought of the pit trap. The gate. The turpentine.

All so intentional. So calculating.

If Jane was insane, then she was getting some form of external direction...possessed by a demon, as would have befit her diabolical actions. That was about as likely as seeing the ghost of Barbie's aunt.

Or, at this point, of seeing Barbie's ghost.

Hammer gripped all the tighter in her free hand, Dawn turned away from Barbie's dead body and raked her gaze around the chapel. There was no sign of the disguised McDonnell anywhere that Dawn could see. Even so, she remained prudent and kept an eye out around the room while dragging Barbie's purse from beneath her corpse.

Dawn fished through it without looking and found two sets of keys by touch alone. One belonged to Kevin, and one belonged to Barbara. Dawn took both along with her because Kevin's keys had that small flashlight on them, and Barbara wasn't going to need it anymore.

Flipping the flashlight on and off, Dawn mentally thanked her friends for managing to get this to her even after death. Its beam even caught something she hadn't fully noticed before. Now she remembered trying to see the Christ statue with the lighter on her first visit to the chapel. Raising the flashlight, she illuminated the same withered dead body that had made Barbara scream.

Dawn felt next to nothing, which was somewhat alarming. The part that bothered her was that this nearly mummified husk of a dead female body had been hanging there an hour or two ago, back when Dawn was innocent and none of this had happened. There it had been, lurking in the shadows, waiting for her to notice.

Shaking her head, Dawn shut off the flashlight.

Then, still with Bongo in her hand, Dawn made her way back to the office with the grandfather clock.

The way seemed longer than ever before. Knowing the truth demystified her fear, but it had come at the cost of a far more terrible knowledge.

Unless Andrea remained unaccounted for because she was going to surprise her by popping out of a closet or arriving with the cavalry, Dawn was the last person standing.

In a way, there was no more reason for her to stay. She had resolved to remain only to help her friends. That strategy had not paid off.

But...Dawn was only human. Humans were subject to powerful emotions. And, of all emotions felt by all humans, one of the most powerful was love.

When damaged by an outside party, love turned rapidly to notions of revenge. In the absence of love, burning hatred raged in Dawn's pained heart. An obligation weighed upon her: one that felt somehow ancient in impulse and design. A primitive instinct blossomed. It informed her that she needed to balance the deaths of her friends with the death of their murderer.

She had already decided that she would not die in this horrible place.

But Jane McDonnell absolutely would.

In the dark office, Dawn set Bongo down beside the gears upon the desk. Hands free, she busied herself in pulling the clock from its place. With the flashlight propped against the doll's arm, Dawn swapped between the screwdriver taken from Chris's body, the wrench she nabbed from the utility closet, and the hammer that was the only tool she intended to keep with her. The rest were abandoned as she used them, and in fact when she was done she did not even bother shutting the little door she had opened to replace the corroded gear.

Simply relieved to know that the gears from the scale fit the clock at all, Dawn stepped around to the face of the clock. Per the instructions in the letter, she turned it back to 4:00.

And, much as she expected, the thing chimed four long, loud times.

That was all right. That was all right. After stuffing Bongo into a drawer of the desk for the moment, Dawn stepped out into the hall with the hammer in her hand.

Just as she shut the broken door behind her, a footstep caught her attention. She looked down the hall.

Jane McDonnell stood at the end, her disguise gone, her face scratched red—from Barbara's attempts at self-defense, Dawn assumed.

The hammer trembled with its wielder's anger.

"Dawn," said Mrs. McDonnell in a relieved tone, stepping down the hall toward her. "I'm so glad to see you. Was that the safe room opening?"

How hard it was to make herself reply! What Dawn wanted to do more than anything was rush forward and smash 'Janie's' face in. Her soul yearned for vengeance; for justice.

And in the name of those ideals, Dawn had to stay calm. She had to look Jane in the face and try to remember what it was like to do so before she knew the truth.

"Mrs. McDonnell! Yes, I think that was it."

With a faint smile, Jane stepped toward her. Dawn tried not to flinch. "You're so smart, Dawn," said Mrs. McDonnell in approval. Mock or real, there was no way to tell. "Maybe when the storm clears we can escape this place together. Where's the safe room?"

"I think it's off the kitchen. Have you found Janie yet?"

Mrs. McDonnell's face fell.

"No," she said softly. "No."

It was so hard to say whether or not Mrs. McDonnell was a victim of her own mind. While, outside, Dawn swore she detected the subtle easing of the storm, she told the woman in a tone not unsympathetic, "I hope that awful nun didn't get her."

Face drawn, Mrs. McDonnell nodded slowly and stared off into space. Not at Dawn, but somewhere to Dawn's left. "I hope not. I'm very scared for her. Very scared of the Mother." Shaking her head, the woman went on, "I even lost Bongo somewhere again. You haven't seen him around, have you?"

"No, Mrs. McDonnell," said Dawn, focused on keeping her voice casual and even. "I haven't."

The furrows of her brow deepened their ravines. Jane hurried toward Dawn, who cringed until the woman reached out to set a hand upon her forearm.

Staring into Dawn's eyes, Jane said, "You'll bring him to the safe room for me if you find him, won't you?"

"I will, Mrs. McDonnell. Right now, I'm going to go find Barbara and lead her there. If I see Bongo on the way, I'll bring him with us."

Nodding, satisfied, Jane released her light grip on Dawn and turned to make her way down the hall.

When she disappeared around the corner, Dawn exhaled with slow relief.

If she was understanding everything— everything—correctly, the nun was getting its information from Jane. Whether Jane was a willful antagonist or coping with a split personality as the result of her trauma, (and, from some of the vile things in that old diary and the vast difference between Jane and the nun, the latter somehow seemed more likely in these impossible circumstances), whatever Jane learned, the nun knew. For instance: Jane learned that it was Scott who had fallen for the turpentine trap; the nun used that information to drop the match on him instead of Dawn.

Therefore, with Jane's knowledge of the safe room, it was now likely that the nun would cloister herself inside it. There, lying in wait, she would be ready for Dawn to arrive and kill her without question or effort. It would be horrible.

Time would pass. Sooner or later, the nun would have an opportunity to do it all again.

All of this was why, after discovering the identity of the nun, Dawn had no more intention of going to the safe room. Instead, the safe room had become a convenient place to trick the nun into putting herself for at least a little while.

At least long enough to find a location allowing something close to an even fight.

When Mrs. McDonnell was out of sight, Dawn crept back into the office—this time, without opening the door. She contorted through the broken window as she had the first time and quietly removed Bongo from the drawer, free to have him on her person now that she knew where Mrs. McDonnell was. It seemed to her, after all, that she was going to need something to bargain or lure the nun in some way. What better than Janie's precious toy?

Next, thinking all the while of locations in the school with only one exit and a fairly level playing field, Dawn hurried to the courtyard door and worked nails free from the boards barring entry. The problem with the school was that it was all interconnected, yet the multiple staircases made navigating it difficult.

Maybe she could somehow trick the nun into

falling in her own razor wire trap? So far as Dawn's vision went, the boards were meant as a bridge over Mary's body...but maybe, when they were arranged, Dawn could wait until the nun was just about to cross, then find a means to pull them away?

Dawn was on the fence about how to corner the nun at all until she got the third board off of the door. She very nearly took the boards to the razor wire trap without looking in the courtyard, but curiosity got the better of her.

A good thing that it did.

The door swung wide and Dawn marveled at the one location in the whole school that seemed suited to her needs. A broad area with space to run in any direction, but enclosed and lacking obstructions.

A location for a fair fight.

In fact, the only obstacles that she could see were, to her surprise, large headstones carved of gray granite. Each was somewhat austere and woefully neglected, but the size of each—as high as Dawn's waist and about twice as wide—indicated the importance of those buried there. She stepped out into the rain and bent before one, peering through the downpour to make out the worn text on the face of the oldest stone.

Mother Cecilia
1792-1866

So the Mother Superiors were buried on-site! How was that for discomforting? Shuddering to imagine going to school with a bunch of dead bodies on the premises—let alone sleeping in such a place every night!—Dawn looked around further. Only one grave seemed to be particularly amiss.

In fact, it was empty.

Dawn shone the flashlight into the empty pit where a grave once stood. No casket sat at the bottom of the hole; no vault or anything else. It were as though whomever had lain here had been buried straight in the earth, without any of the normal funeral accoutrements.

The light's beam trailed up. No headstone.

If Dawn had been a betting woman, she would have ventured a guess that this grave belonged to Mother Apollonia...and that this was the identity of the missing nun mentioned in the story about this awful place.

Dawn felt a pang of something close to fear again.

It was relieving, in a way. She wasn't completely numb to all that was happening around her.

The dead body crucified in the chapel must have been Apollonia. It hadn't been enough to turn Apollonia's violence outward upon the rest of the boarding school, evidently...Janie had been forced to become Apollonia. To exhume her body and rob it of its clothes. To kill while bearing the Mother Superior's identity.

With a shudder, Dawn set Bongo before the grave and left to find a shovel.

11.

MRS. MCDONNELL DRIFTED through the halls of St. Cecilia's like a phantom. Bongo! Oh, poor Bongo. Where were you?

If Mrs. McDonnell couldn't find her Janie, at least she might manage to find Bonago. The trouble was that she wasn't sure where she'd dropped him. After running around the school the whole night, practically turning it upside-down in search of a lost little girl, Mrs. McDonnell wasn't even sure where to look for the old toy.

Better to start from the beginning. Retrace her steps. Where had she been earlier in the night?

She remembered finding the teenagers in the dining hall. Since she needed to go to the kitchen and see if there really was a safe room that had opened, it seemed a prudent place to check first. Her body tensed in anticipation for any unexpected noise, Mrs. McDonnell retraced her steps back through the school.

The Mother Superior's first victim that night had been the nice-looking young man. His stomach now writhed with the rats that had eaten their way inside of him and presently gorged themselves on his innards. It looked like his corpse was about to explode.

The sight made Mrs. McDonnell retch. Covering her mouth, glancing away, the woman hurried through to the kitchen and consoled herself that Bongo was nowhere to be seen in the dining hall.

Nor was he anywhere in the kitchen...but Dawn was right. A safe room had, in fact, opened up off of the kitchen. One of the walls had disappeared to reveal a white passage into some room beyond. Mrs. McDonnell wanted to go in and take a look at it, but once she was there she feared she would be tempted to remain...and she couldn't do that until she found Bongo.

Besides...maybe, just maybe, this would be when she found Janie.

Why had Janie ever been sent to a place like this? It just wasn't fair. Mrs. McDonnell didn't know what she was thinking at the time. Janie was such a bright, happy, free-spirited girl. A little bit of a trouble-maker, of course. Not always the proper sort of girl one expected a young lady of her age to be.

But had she deserved to come to a place like this? A place where students were beaten with rulers and locked in solitary confinement when they disobeyed the rules?

Mrs. McDonnell thought of the folder she found in that office after talking to the tall girl. The manila tab had been printed with Janie's name, and Mrs. McDonnell had read it all end to end right there in the office. She had been so upset after seeing the contents of the so-called "incident reports" that she had torn the papers up and thrown them into the trash with angry tears in her eyes.

This evil Mother Apollonia woman, she had done things to poor Janie. Terrible things. The other girls hadn't been treated the way Janie was treated. Janie was a good girl.

Why didn't God care about her? Why didn't her mother care about her?

Janie even liked to pray. While, in search of Bongo, she wandered the halls to the office, Janie prayed to herself in a whisper.

"The Lord is my light and my salvation. Whom shall I fear? The Lord is the strength of my life. Of whom shall I be afraid? Hide not Thy face far from me. Put not thy servant away in anger. Thou hast been my help. Leave me not, neither forsake me, O God of my salvation, for He gives me the power to always see Thee."

It was sad that Mrs. McDonnell would never find Janie. That wasn't really either of their faults. It was all the Mother's fault. The Mother was just so cruel! There was nothing she loved more than keeping the two of them apart. Janie could have been standing right in front of Mrs. McDonnell, right there in the mirror, and Mrs. McDonnell wouldn't have seen it if the Mother wouldn't allow her to.

That was all right, though.

Janie understood how to take care of herself.

She understood, too, how to protect herself from the Mother.

Bongo could help protect her from the Mother, too. If only she knew where he was! He liked to hide this way sometimes, but Janie could usually find him. He wasn't in the office where Mrs. McDonnell met that tall girl, though. And when she went to take a look on the stairs, he wasn't there, either! There was just another dead guy, another victim of the Mother, looking wide-eyed with terror in a sticky soup of his own mostly dried blood.

Janie wrinkled her nose and made her way down the stairs again. Mrs. McDonnell couldn't handle seeing a thing like that, but Janie had an iron stomach—and, when she was focused on a goal, she tended to see it through in a very single-minded fashion. What was the point, after all, in worrying about dead people? They were already dead.

And it wasn't like the Mother could hurt Janie. Apollonia had hurt Janie a lot, often, very badly. Apollonia had been a snide and hateful woman—a sinner of the highest, most inexcusable order. Imagine, treating a child with such cruelty!

Moreover, treating a child with such cruelty when other children were passed over. Mother had been outraged to see such a thing. It had only been natural that she arrived to protect poor Janie! After all: Janie had been abandoned. Trapped in this hellish excuse for a school. Everyone had been very surprised to meet the Mother, but they shouldn't have been.

They earned her attention. They deserved her attention. If there was one thing to be learned at St. Cecilia's Preparatory School, it was that no one could be trusted in this world.

Mother found herself without her habit and went to go fetch it from its hiding place in the shower room. Only in the garments of her uniform did she feel natural, at peace. Once her gloves were on, Mother took the stairs down to see if Janie's toy had fallen by the edge of the landing pit.

There was no sign of the little clown there. Only a dead redhead whose blood had since stopped dripping from her slit throat.

Mother stood at the end of the upstairs hallway and considered where else she had been that night.

The boy. The boy she had almost caught by the edge of the pit, who then was later set ablaze. Had Janie dropped her toy while he was streaking down the hallway like a human ball of fire?

Mother was always picking up after Janie—and herself, of course. It was why Mrs. McDonnell just couldn't understand.

There was no evidence of anything to understand. This was by design. Otherwise, Janie would be imperiled. In order to protect little Janie's existence, Mother made sure that Mrs. McDonnell could never find any evidence of what had been done while she wasn't looking.

Though they did see one another from time to time, Mrs. McDonnell and Mother. Sometimes, when Janie couldn't come out of hiding and ease back down to earth as Jane, Mrs. McDonnell awoke so sharply that she became aware of the presence of the nun. Fear and paranoia would surge over her. For days on end she would eschew the basic necessities of her own health in order to hide from the nun that she was sure would glide out from around every and any corner to claim her life.

In such a situation, only Bongo seemed capable of tethering her to the ground again...and only because his presence reminded little Janie that the nun was there to help her. The nun existed to protect Janie. As long as Mrs. McDonnell cared about Janie, she had nothing to fear.

The classroom—the one where the boy's charred corpse hung halfway out of the school, impaled upon the glass shards of the window through which he tried to leap—contained no clown toy. Only evidence that the storm was beginning to abate.

If Mother was going to protect Janie from interlopers and what they could persuade Mrs. McDonnell to do, (go to the police or a hospital, start medication, even kill herself), then Mother needed to take care of the final girl.

But Janie yearned too sharply for the comfort of her toy. And so Mother paused a moment, staring through the blackened corpse. She thought of where else she had been.

Ah, the chapel. The girl who had been martyred in the fashion of Saint Lucy, little Janie's favorite saint. Even Apollonia had been there for that one. Maybe that was where Bongo had gotten to! Yes...all the grasping and thrashing about that young woman did, surely that was it.

Knife already in her hand in case she should meet the living girl, Mother glided steadily through the dark halls of the school. She intended to fetch Bongo and go straight to the safe room to take care of the chatty little fool who had finally revealed its location to her after all these years of curiosity...but something caught her attention while she passed from one wing to the other.

The boards had been removed from the courtyard door.

Mother had put those up years ago to prove to Apollonia she would have no rest. Once those who looked gave up any search for Janie or Apollonia, Mother dug up the dead abuser of innocent children and mounted her where she belonged. After all! Had Apollonia not shown Janie how vile even a nun could be, Mother would never have existed.

It seemed important, therefore, that Apollonia know what she did...and even more important that Apollonia know she would never be permitted to rest.

That was why the absence of the boards inspired awful terror in Janie. Was something bad going to happen? The girl's heart raced.

Poor thing. Mother couldn't stand to see Janie so afraid. Intent on assuaging that fear, she stepped into the subsiding rain. The girl simply needed to remember her prayers.

"The Lord is my light and my salvation. Whom shall I fear?"

Yes, yes. That was very good. Mother made her way toward the empty grave of Apollonia to prove to Janie that nothing could hurt them. No monster had burst from the earth to enact some vengeance on behalf of the dead headmistress.

Something did sit before the pit, however.

Janie continued to recite in a fast whisper.

"The Lord is the strength of my life. Of whom shall I be afraid?"

Rain beat upon Mother's face while she stopped at the edge of Apollonia's grave.

"Hide not Thy face far from me. Put not Thy servant away in anger."

Bongo smiled up at her.

Janie's heart overflowed with delight but Mother recoiled a step, whipping around with the chef's knife held high. Focused on Bongo as she was, Janie prayed even as Dawn's shovel swung at her.

"Thou hast been my help. Leave me not, neither forsake me, O God of my salvation, for He gives me the power to always see Thee."

The knife flew from Mother's hand and down into the grave.

18.

DAWN HAD BEEN lucky that Jane hadn't seen or heard her in the rain.

She had crouched behind the headstone right before Apollonia's open grave, the shovel from the downstairs utility closet gripped in trembling fists. It had been an obvious risk to sit outside with an implement of metal and wood while a thunderstorm raged, but by the time she was back up from the basement and ready to position herself in the courtyard, the storm had begun to well and truly settle.

Almost like nature itself wanted Jane McDonnell dead.

Bolstered by this thought, Dawn focused on remaining as still as possible. She waited, and waited, and tried not to tremble.

Eventually, the door opened.

Jane McDonnell stepped out into the courtyard.

Dawn couldn't look to confirm that she had changed into her nun costume, but the fast-paced and somehow desperate whispering she produced was almost as reliable an indicator of this heinous condition. Slowly, the whispering grew louder. So did the squelch of mud beneath feet.

Dawn's grip tightened around the shovel.

Would the so-called nun catch sight of her? If she didn't, would it matter? Jane was incredibly fast when she needed to be.

And she was certainly fast there in the courtyard... but that didn't change the fact that, with another stroke of luck, the knife was knocked from the nun's hand when it made contact with the shovel's head.

A short spark of joy lit Dawn's heart, but she didn't let it distract her. Instead, more focused than ever in her life, she drew the shovel back and swung again at the madwoman. The woman who had murdered all of Dawn's closest friends.

The nun was too fast.

Jane dodged the blow and grabbed hold of the shovel. At close range, each with her own grip on the implement, Dawn stared into Jane McDonnell's face. Empty eyes gazed back, framed within the shadows of the veil.

"Mrs. McDonnell," she said, "Jane—please, stop doing this! Why would you want to hurt innocent people like this?"

Nothing changed in the nun's dark face. There was not even any sign of animal bloodlust there. Only those matte, empty eyes that stared dully as though through Dawn were a phantom.

The only change was a slight tension that appeared with the exertion required to finally jerk the shovel from Dawn's hands.

Crying out, Dawn stumbled back and caught herself on the edge of the headstone. The hammer in her back pocket clanged against the granite and she took a breath, snatching it out to wield it with her free hand extended before her.

"Please, Mrs. McDonnell! You don't have to do this. Do you realize that you're Janie? That you and Janie and this nun are all the same person?"

The nun drew the shovel back with the wide sweep of a baseball player and slammed a home run against Dawn's extended hand.

Dawn's scream was no match for the crunch of her bones. Her right hand would never be the same again after that night. For the most part, it would look fine; but the loss in finger dexterity would be doomed to change her interest in writing and playing music to an interest in conducting.

And every time it rained, she would feel the pain, and remember Jane McDonnell.

The white flames of agony passed over Dawn's consciousness to find she had stumbled some steps to the left. Jane had dropped the shovel and taken the opportunity to slide down into the empty grave. While her shattered hand swelled and her still-functioning left one began to sweat amid the severity of the pain, Dawn saw she had one chance.

While the nun bent to pick up the knife, Dawn slid into the grave with the hammer at the ready. Stumbling down to the ground, unable to balance herself with her broken hand, Dawn blindly waved the hammer and made hard contact with the side of

Mrs. McDonnell's knee.

The nun's voice raised in tremulous agony, her prolonged scream full of rage.

Dawn staggered to her feet while her opponent slammed against the muddy wall of the grave, then slid upright against it to turn around and catch the hammer before it fell again. With two hands, Jane stayed Dawn and left the teenager struggling to compensate for her own one-handed condition.

"Mrs. McDonnell, please. You can't want to do this, can you? You can't want to kill me. It's something else inside of you."

Jane extricated the hammer from Dawn's grip and threw it. While it bounced to the foot of the grave, the woman dressed as a nun threw herself upon Dawn and gripped her by the throat.

Rasping, Dawn remembered what had been done to Barbie. Her teeth grit as she lifted her thumbs to thrust them into McDonnell's eyes. Jane cried out, her eyelids squeezing sharply shut and her face contorting in pain. While she released Dawn and countered this by gripping her broken hand until Dawn quite literally collapsed from the agony, the music student still tried talking sense into her assailant. She lay on her back in the mud, cradling her wounded hand once McDonnell released it—and still, she talked.

"You've been looking for Janie all this time, Mrs. McDonnell, but I found her! I found Janie. She's right here!"

McDonnell paused, frozen while bending with the rain-slickened knife reclaimed in her hand. She searched Dawn's face as Dawn went on, "Janie's okay, Mrs. McDonnell. She's safe. And she'll be safe...or will be, when the nun is gone."

The killer said nothing.

She raised the knife, poised to stab Dawn.

"Please—please, Janie isn't safe from the nun! If you let her stay, sooner or later you'll end up in an asylum. Then Janie will be taken away from you forever, Mrs. McDonnell! Janie, and Bongo."

The knife paused, quivering.

Somehow, in some strange and almost indiscernible way, Jane's face changed.

"Somebody wants to take Bongo away?"

Exhaling, lowering the broken hand that had raised to shield her from at least the first few stabs, Dawn stared up at Jane McDonnell.

"Yes," said Dawn softly. "Yes. They'll take everything away...but especially Bongo."

"No"—the grown woman's girlish whimper was terrifying, her chest heaving as she began to endure some kind of panic attack—"no, no. Please, I've been a good girl—"

Here. Here it was.

If Dawn could just push this, she would get what she needed.

Dawn nodded and forced herself to play along.

"I know, Janie. That's why Mrs. McDonnell has been looking all over for you. She wants to save you from the nun. Don't you, Mrs. McDonnell? Jane? Don't you want to protect Janie from the nun? You understand, don't you?"

The woman's lips trembled. Dawn pressed on.

"Don't you?"

With a mute sob, Jane's eyes squeezed shut. She nodded, dropped the knife with a groan, and soon enough fell weeping to her knees in the bottom of Mother Apollonia's grave.

"They won't leave me alone," screamed Mrs. McDonnell, her hands balling into fists around the fabric of her black veil. "I just can't escape this place! No matter what I try, I end up back here—I always end up back here. Back with them."

"I know, Mrs. McDonnell," said Dawn softly.

While McDonnell covered her face with a piteous sob, Dawn picked the hammer up with her good hand.

"I just want to be a good person," Mrs. McDonnell continued between desperate gasps for air. "I just want to control myself. I don't—I don't—I don't want to do these things. I'm so afraid! I'm so afraid of her. Of what she makes me do."

"It's okay, Mrs. McDonnell."

Clambering uneasily to her feet, Dawn steadied herself against the side of the grave and raised the hammer.

"No, it's not. I—I killed those people. The nun inside me killed those people. I just don't know how I can make her stop!"

"I do," said Dawn while swinging the hammer upon the top of McDonnell's black veil.

The cracks of Jane McDonnell's skull beneath the head of the hammer were the final bursts of thunder the mountain would hear that night. One, two, three blows rained upon McDonnell's head. By the time the third lifted away, the violent nun swayed upon her knees. At long last, she keeled face-first into the dirt.

Panting, Dawn dropped the hammer. She turned to climb out of the grave. Mud slipped beneath her hand and the forearm she threw up over the edge of the pit. Her shoes stuck in the gloppy sides.

Mrs. McDonnell grabbed her ankle and tried to pull her back down into the darkness.

A cry lifted from Dawn's lips. She struggled, kicking, and made hard contact with the spot on the back of McDonnell's head where the hammer had fallen so many times.

The nun released her.

Dawn escaped Apollonia's grave.

Rolling out upon her back and gasping for breath, Dawn permitted herself the luxury of only a few seconds to breathe in the promising air of accomplishment.

Still had to finish the job, though.

Could Dawn kill the nun herself, in a direct way?

No. Not really.

Even after all that had happened, the young woman just couldn't stand the thought of ending a human life with her own two hands.

But she couldn't dream of leaving McDonnell alive.

So, she did all that she could do.

Spade of earth by spade of earth, with the swollen wrist of her broken hand braced beneath the shovel, Dawn filled in Apollonia's grave.

The stuff she tossed into the pit was more like a slurry of mud and gravel than it was solid dirt. That somehow seemed better. Like if she could pack it densely enough, the job would be done faster. The job of Jane McDonnell's death, that was...the actual act of burial would take quite some time.

But Dawn was patient, and steady.

When committing to some monotonous task like folding laundry or sorting her albums, it alway amazed her how quickly such things could pass. The act of repetition seemed to inspire a kind of trance. One scoop at a time, Dawn tossed muddy earth into the grave and atop the body of Mrs. McDonnell.

One scoop at a time, Dawn was closer to true free-dom.

Jane stirred, still face-down in the grave. Moaning in pain, she began to sit up when the pressure upon her broken knee made it apparent such a thing was impossible.

"Oh"—the alarming, girlish tone of Janie had lifted back to her voice, a pathetic whine accompanied by a sudden onslaught of tears—"please, please let me out! I didn't do anything wrong...I just want to go home. I don't know why I'm here."

Lips pressed thin, Dawn kept filling in the grave.

"Where's Bongo? Did you take Bongo from me? Help! Someone help me! Please, someone help me—I don't want to die."

"Neither did my friends," said Dawn darkly, throwing this pile of dirt in with a bit of extra malice. "Neither did all the people at the boarding school."

"But Mother Apollonia—"

"It doesn't matter what Mother Apollonia did to you," Dawn deigned to answer, her motions never ceasing. The constant rhythm of the spade sinking into earth and depositing it with a splat into the grave remained unfaltering beneath her words. "No matter how horrible she was, you had no right to take her life along with the lives of anybody else in this school. You had no right to try to kill me."

"But I didn't do it! Please! It was the Mother. Please, don't punish me for something she did."

For just a second, Dawn's heart weakened.

The second passed.

She redoubled her efforts.

Jane McDonnell sobbed beneath the dirt, especially as it began to cover her head. "There is no way to control this child," she whimpered to herself. "No, no. I'm a good girl, a good girl. She doesn't treat the other kids this way."

Then, unnervingly, Jane's voice assumed a new and sharper tone. The tone of an old woman, rather than a young girl or a woman of her true age.

"Say your prayers," she whispered sharply. "Say your prayers, child. It's the only way. Pray for the sinner. Pray for Mother."

In a tone so hushed it was almost impossible to hear, Jane prayed while the grave filled in over her.

"The Lord is my light and my salvation. Whom shall I fear? The Lord is the strength of my life. Of whom shall I be afraid? Hide not Thy face far from me. Put not Thy servant away in anger. Thou hast been my help. Leave me not, neither forsake me, O God of my salvation, for He gives me the power to always see Thee."

Even when the dirt completely covered her back, Dawn could still hear the woman reciting.

"The Lord is my light and my salvation. Whom shall I fear? The Lord is the strength of my life. Of whom shall I be afraid? Hide not Thy face far from me. Put not Thy servant away in anger. Thou hast been my help. Leave me not, neither forsake me, O God of my salvation, for He gives me the power to always see Thee."

Several inches now stood between her and Jane McDonnell. Still the telltale prayer rose up. Weakly, stifled, the words choked by dirt and lack of air—but audible.

"The Lord is my light and my salvation. Whom shall I fear? The Lord is the strength of my life. Of whom shall I be afraid? Hide not Thy face far from me.

Put not Thy servant away in anger. Thou hast been my help. Leave me not, neither forsake me, O God of my salvation, for He gives me the power to always see Thee."

The final repetition came as Dawn filled the hole nearly to the top. By then, the storm had ceased. Morning seemed close, though she had lost all sense of time and could no longer be sure how long she had spent amid this ordeal.

"The Lord is—my light and my salvation. Whom shall...I fear? The Lord is the—is the strength of my life. Of...whom shall I be afraid? Hide not Thy face..."

Dawn waited for the rest.

It never came.

She filled the grave higher, until the earth was a mound on top of the spot where Jane McDonnell had taken the place of Mother Apollonia.

Dawn stared down at it, listening for any sign of life.

None came.

19.

DAWN WAITED IN the courtyard for an hour to be sure Jane McDonnell wouldn't crawl out of the grave any time soon.

She never wanted to do this again.

Once, when Dawn's father had worked the night shift for a week, she had come home from school to find him washing dishes as though it were nothing.

"What are you doing up? Shouldn't you be sleeping right now?"

"I'm too exhausted to be exhausted," was his answer.

For the first time, Dawn understood that concept perfectly. The idea of collapsing on the spot seemed somehow alluring...but there was still more to do. Always more to do.

Body aching, mind thick with the fog of constant exertion and long hours of panic, Dawn limped out of the courtyard and back through the school. The shovel, she left there. The knife and the hammer remained down in the grave with Mrs. McDonnell. She brought with her one single thing only.

Dawn wasn't sure what she was going to tell authorities when they questioned her, but she honestly didn't care.

After all that had happened, this was the least Jane McDonnell deserved.

Dawn stepped out of St. Cecilia's Preparatory School through the same door where they entered. The soft, pinkish glow of morning winked from the east and provided just enough light for her to begin a slow descent down the mountain road.

It was a good thing they waited. More chunks of the ancient highway had eroded. More than once she had to edge along the remaining bit of cliff. To hope her fate was not to survive the night only to die on the mountain.

Fortune was with her, however. The growing sunlight made the hike a simple if prolonged matter; the road was still a bit slick, but fast to dry once the daytime was well-installed.

After a steady trek of just over an hour, she reached Barbie's car with something close to a sob of relief.

Her good hand opened the car door. Her bad hand threw her trophy into the passenger's side.

Slumping back in the driver's seat, Dawn inhaled, exhaled, inhaled, exhaled. The warm buzz of adrenal afterglow made her body heavy; made reality seem unreal. She sat there like a zombie for a few long minutes, still in disbelief about all that had happened.

She looked down at herself. Her clothes were covered in blood. The only reason her hands didn't match was because of all the rain, she supposed—though dirt blackened the beds of all her nails as a suitable substitute.

After looking around through Barbie's car, Dawn discovered a light blue cardigan and pulled it on over her head. At the very least, it covered the bloodstained clothes...and smelled like her dead friend, soft and floral perfume mingling with the sad reality that this scent now represented a memory with a terrible ending.

Desperate to get home and go to bed, Dawn started the car, turned it around, and cruised down the mountain.

She was not sure what she was going to do with the car, but the reality of her circumstances emphasized themselves to her when the roadblock appeared about another mile of driving later. Her jaw tightened. If only these clowns had been around the night before, a little higher up the mountain! Maybe somebody might have been there to help her friends...somebody, anybody other than her.

Instead, Dawn had been forced to sacrifice herself.

Yes. Some fundamental part of her mind, her soul—something once rooted in the very core of her personality no longer seemed to be there, although she could not say just what it was.

Dawn slowed the car at the direction of the highway patrol officers setting up the roadblock. As she rolled down the window, one approached with the collar of his jacket pulled around his face to protect him from the mountain chill.

What was she going to say? What was she going to

say to this man? How was she going to explain what happened up there?

"Excuse me, ma'am—how'd you get up here? The pass is closed due to erosion, there's been a landslide."

For some reason, a tiny voice in the back of Dawn's head compelled her to lie.

"Oh," she said in mock surprise, glancing back over her shoulder and up the mountain road. As he followed her gaze she stole the opportunity to pull the sleeve of Barbie's cardigan over her swollen hand, an action that caused her tremendous pain. She fought against it while casually asking, "Really? I was camping all night."

The man arched a brow. "In the rain?"

"It wasn't raining when I went up, sir...but it started once I made it, and I didn't want to drive back down. Stayed in my car all night and waited for it to dry off."

With a slight sniff, the cop said, "Well, that was probably a good idea, but if you're going to go camping then you should know it's just not safe to do it alone these days. You never know what's going to happen—a lot of people go missing in America every year, especially out in the wilderness."

Nodding solemnly, Dawn said, "You're not kidding."

A spark of inspiration filled her. Gesturing back up the mountain with her good hand, she lied, "When I was camping, I saw a Jeep full of people go driving up even higher than I was. I don't know if it was safe for them to go so far, but I didn't have a chance to flag them down."

With a quick, grave look at his nearby partner, the cop questioning Dawn asked, "When was this?"

"Oh, I don't know...something like ten or so last night."

His blue eyes searching her face, he went on to inquire, "And they didn't come back down?"

Dawn shook her head. "Not that I saw."

The cop's nostrils flared. He looked at his partner and waved a hand. Dawn tried not to look too relieved when said partner temporarily set aside the striped barrier they'd been assigned to place. "And my partner over there thought today was going to be no problem...sounds like we might be in for some overtime. Thanks for letting us know, young lady...be extremely careful if you keep camping by yourself."

"Thank you, officer," she said with as pleasant a smile as she could manage.

Beginning to relax at long last, Dawn cruised through the roadblock, waved at the second officer, and resumed the drive back to town.

There was still over an hour to go. Over an hour to think and wonder. How would she be able to look her family in the face again? How could she have any kind of future when her friends were dead? Dead. Dead!

And her, alive.

Dawn could still barely believe it. The weight of her continued existence seemed somehow significant. It made her all the more driven to excel in life.

Yet, when carrying this kind of trauma, excelling would surely be a tall order. Dawn was going to have to figure a lot of things out. She had to determine how to cope with her new vision of the world—and her new vision of herself.

Because, though she may not have killed Jane McDonnell with her own two hands, Dawn couldn't lie to herself the way she had to the cops.

Couldn't lie to herself the way Jane had.

That was what trauma did to those helplessly

disarmed by its staggering weight. Trauma broke open the present space and brought the harsh, hateful reality of the past springing back before the faces of the traumatized. Even in the car, even when she passed the *Welcome* sign of her quaint hometown, Dawn felt ready for something to go wrong. Felt ready for the nun to spring out of the back seat and slit her throat across the dashboard.

Instead, Barbie's compact car cruised into town. Suburbia was just starting to awaken on that lazy Sunday morning. Beneath the bright blue sky, manicured lawns glowed with the jade of stubbornly clutched rain drops. The time was almost eleven, though hard-working fathers were just now stumbling out in their plush robes and worn slippers to collect newspapers protruding from their bushes.

Church had ended, and parishioners in their Sunday best poured out along the sidewalk to the adjacent parking lot.

Averting her eyes, Dawn drove on.

She left the car not too far from the church, on the other side of town from her house. In it, she abandoned Barbara's cardigan and Kevin's keys. The only thing she took was the item that sat with her in the passenger's seat. It fit perfectly in the crook of her wounded arm as she made her slow and steady way across town.

Passersby stared. She wasn't sure if they were looking at her broken hand, or the blood staining her shirt, or what she carried.

She didn't really care. Consequences could come later. For now, she was safe.

It felt good to walk through town. Felt good, so good, to hear the chirping of birds and watch the passing of neighbors' cars. Lawn mowers. Radios. Friends chatting over fences. Bells ringing on kids' bikes. Dogs barking at her passage.

The music of eternity: her reward for holding on to life.

It sort of amazed Dawn somehow that she had managed to retain her own set of keys during the ordeal. Upon fishing them from her pocket with her left hand, Dawn opened the back door of the house and slipped into the kitchen.

The safe, familiar sounds of her father tinkering away on model airplanes rose up to her ears from the basement. Dawn slipped off her shoes and, with her newfound skill for sneaking, crept quietly through the living room. A note from her mother sat on the telephone stand.

Welcome home, Dawn!

I hope you had fun with your friends. Just ran to the store, back soon.

Love, Mom
XOXO

PS: We're having steak tonight!

That hollow core of Dawn's essential self almost warmed to read the note. She took it with her while making her way up the stairs, feeling only the slightest bit bad about her intentions to lie to her parents. They would believe her, though, and defend her to the cops if she needed defending. They would happily tell officers that she had actually been home all night, having been driven back and dropped off by Kevin when she'd gotten a bad feeling about the thunderstorm.

It was just that they didn't hear her come in because they were asleep, and they never thought to look in her shut bedroom because she was supposed to be elsewhere that night.

And her hand? Well...she slipped and fell on it on her way into the house. An accident that wouldn't have happened if she had just stayed with her friends! Yes...the ER bill and rehab costs would be a pittance compared to what would have happened if she had remained up there on the mountain, her parents would soon enough find.

Everything would sort itself out as if by design.

Her hand throbbing worse than ever, Dawn set her memento upon her dresser. She swiftly took the maximum dose of aspirin, undressed, and enjoyed the most relieving shower of her life. The events of the night felt like a movie she had seen many years before. None of it would feel real until she had gotten a night of sleep and woke up to find reality unchanged.

Wrapped in a robe, Dawn filled the bathtub halfway and left her sneakers there to soak. She would throw them in the washer later.

For now, she needed sleep.

Ignoring the sound of her mother arriving home downstairs, Dawn perched upon the edge of her twin-sized bed. It felt like the bed of a child she'd never met. She ran her thumb blearily along the threadbare sheets she'd slept on since she was thirteen.

She lifted her head.

The stuffed clown stared at her from where he sat on the edge of her dresser.

Dawn almost smirked before she realized she didn't have the strength. At the very least, she managed to speak.

"I guess I owe you one for all this, huh, pal?"

Bongo smiled on.

That time, he didn't reply.

PUPPET COMBO®

Influenced by slasher movies and low-poly survival horror titles from the PS1 and PS2 eras of gaming, Puppet Combo® is a prolific studio whose titles range from such nightmarish offerings like POWER DRILL MASSACRE to the more conceptually surreal FEED ME, BILLY. NUN MASSACRE is the company's second collaborative novelization: be sure to look for BABYSITTER BLOODBATH! Check out Puppet Combo®'s website for more on its games, including NUN MASSACRE—then, support the creation of new games (and get tons of fantastic content) by contributing to their Patreon.

REGINA WATTS

Regina Watts is an author of horror and sf/f fiction, and a longtime fan of Puppet Combo®'s games. Be sure to explore Regina's work on Amazon—especially her BABYSITTER BLOODBATH adaptation, or her serialized splatterpunk horrotica, DOTTIE FOR YOU. Get free stories by signing up for her newsletter, and don't be shy about leaving a nice Amazon review if you enjoyed NUN MASSACRE: it's an easy way to help both creators at the same time!

Printed in Great Britain
by Amazon